MW01173529

THE ORG

Biography of a Violent Man

It went down on a cold winter's night. It was going down in the building right in front of me. The deal where two small-time drug crews were to meet and discuss plans to unite. They were to join forces and divi up the benefits from their so-called turfs and territories. So my sources revealed. These guys did it all. Extortion, loan sharking, racketeering, kidnapping, murder, etc. That is just to name a few. And all of them were in that one building. But it does not faze me much. I have a deed to fulfill. I am not concerned with what they do, or what they have done. However, a select few of others are. Others, who felt that they have been wronged. Consider a certain group of family members whom decided that they have had just about enough. Yes. But not your typical family if you know what I mean. However, I'll introduce you to them a little later. So who do they get to rectify this problem? Who else, but yours truly? That's right. Send in the tough guy and see if he's worthy enough. And I don't know if I should've been honored that they sent me by myself, or angry that this should've been a suicide mission. The fuck were they trying to pull? I'd show them though. And I'd take it out on these flour heads in that building just for making my employers send me out here in the first place. How do you like that philosophy?

So there I was waiting at a corner bodega. Standing there looking as though I lost something. I have spent about a half of an hour waiting and circling the block now as an attempt to elude suspicion and possible harassment from your local police. With every short trek I tried to keep track of anyone going in or out of the building through the number of cars they had parked outside. They were quite a few colorful and expensive ones at that. Every once in awhile I had to keep repeating to myself that this was for the thrill baby. The currency I was to receive for this job helped me to stay focused as well. All I had for an arsenal was a bulletproof vest complete with iron leg pads, and a fully loaded handgun with two extra clips in my coat pocket. All I needed. I wasn't there to take on an army. It was just one person who was my target, and that target was none other than a guy named Tony "the tomahawk" Texas. He was some hustler from the west who decided to expand his horizons here in the big apple. That family I referred to earlier just wanted to make him into an example. I figured that I'd most likely have to throw in a few others though. As more time passed I felt myself growing more impatient and tense, but soon got a grip when I saw the front doors open.

Out they came into the streets laughing and cracking jokes. Instantly I spotted Tony. He was a slim tough faced looking fellow. He also dressed fancy, donning Shark skinned shoes, black leather suit with a long leather coat to match, hat with the feather and a huge high quality grade platinum ring laced with diamonds. This gentleman was apparently living the good life. Not for long. It was time for me to make the move. I cocked back my peacemaker as they made their way to their vehicles. About seven of them were with him. I put on the ski mask that I had tucked in my coat pocket and started across the street. Tony and two others already got into his car as the others headed for their own. Of course, I made my way to the one that contained Tony. He was in the backseat when I approached. He turned and noticed the toast aimed directly at him. At the same time, he somehow managed to duck instantly as I fired five shots through the car window. I do not know if the first one hit, but I am damn sure that the other four got him something severely. As I backed up I fired four more shots into the front of the car to deter the other goons from jumping out. Just before I turned to run I could not only see guys coming out from the other cars, but from out of the building as well. A barrage of shots rang out at me as I turned the corner. Now I was running full speed down the block like a broad barely escaping a mugger. I'm sweating bullets and I could feel my chest pounding heavy. Did I underestimate the fact that an army of angry killers would be chasing me? They must have hit the block I was on pretty quick too, for I heard shots ring out just before I swung into the alleyway of abandoned buildings. I jumped onto the fire escape ladder and made my way up. As I looked down I spotted only three of them. Only three? The others must have gone a different route. I emptied the remainder of my clip at them striking down one and wounding the other. The one still able returned fire as I jumped into the building. There, I waited for him to come up, but as I slowly peered outside could see him and the other wounded guy running back out the other end. What do I do now? I thought for a moment and then reloaded another clip. I had one extra left now. I went up the stairwell heading for the roof. As soon as I opened the door a shot zipped by barely missing my head. This startled me so that I fell back down the stairs hitting my head on a rusty pipe. Though a little disoriented I had to keep moving. Who knew where else they could be waiting? Fuck it. I'm running out blasting and I will not stop until I am long gone.

I rushed madly down the stairs to another floor as I heard footsteps above me. Forced out onto the fire escape, I found myself heading back down to where I first entered. It was a wild and desperate move. The body I laid there earlier was still in that spot. This was not thrill anymore. This was terror. I continued back through the alleyway from which first entered and came upon a fence that I hopped faster than a bullfrog. Somehow I came up behind two of them. How they didn't hear me approach is still baffling. I didn't want to open fire as it would attract attention, but I had no choice. I was getting closer now and they would surely turn around and notice me. So I fired two into the back of one and ended up in a brief struggle with the other. I backed up tripping over a garbage can as he came right up on me, pistol drawn and squeezed off. Pale I must've turned in the split second that occurred, but I must be the God's nephew for no shots came forth. If he was on empty, then it was time for me to fill him back up again. He fumbled around with his gun trying to figure out what was wrong with it, but he knew it was hopeless. I aimed right at his dome and filled his head full of knowledge. Next time you're reincarnated into this situation – make sure you don't forget to bring a working gun. As he dropped I felt overwhelming relief, but soon realized that more would come with even more bullets now. It was a must that I get off foot.

I reloaded my last clip and continued down the other dark end of the alley. As I entered out onto the other side of the block it was just my luck to happen upon a man about to get into his vehicle. I grabbed him and threw him to the ground pointing the biscuit right at him, just to let him know I meant business. Got the keys off and banged up the car a bit in my haste to get out of the parking space. Just as I was pulling out the opposing group appeared for a couple yards. I started blasting at them as I sped off. They answered back without delay as a barrage of bullets slammed through and into the car smashing the rear windows and cracking the windshield. As I glimpsed through the rear view mirror I could see that one of them shot the guy that I had car-jacked. Apparently they just wanted to kill out of anger or frustration. Once out of sight I took off the mask, which was now damp with sweat and parked the car after only a couple of blocks. I did not want to take the chance of getting pulled over by your local police in a car tagged with fresh new bullet holes. As I slammed the car door the front windshield just shattered. "No finger prints," I thought removing my gloves while heading for the nearest train station.

On the ride home my tension was eased. A sudden rush came over me from the station to my apartment. I reflected on how it all went down. I was sure Tony Texas was no longer with us. As I removed my garments I noticed something startling. There were about three bullets lodged into my armor - two in the leg pads and the one in the upper back of the vest. Could I have been hit and not felt a thing? How is this possible? Was it because I was too tense and pumped on adrenaline? Nah, not just that. It's because I was Non – and this is the Biography of a Violent Man...

Chapter I – Humble beginnings

But how did it all begin? How did I conform into this kind of lifestyle? That's a question I still sometimes ask myself. I guess it began back in 97, two years after I finished high school. Matter of fact, I had dropped out of college a year before cause I just grew tired of the classroom – college – future hype. I had other things in mind. I didn't really know exactly what I wanted to do, but I knew that I was bored with school and just wanted to start working to make some money. I just felt that school wouldn't pay off unless I was going to be a doctor or lawyer or computer programmer or something like that, but these were professions for which I had no desire. I just knew I wanted to run my own thing eventually, but I also knew I had to begin somewhere so I went to look for work. I came back home to the 'Big Apple' and got to it. I started to work fast food. Yeah, fast Food! I was young. But an altercation with the way of things made it so that my employment there was short.

"Ok Non" the manager of the fast food joint started. My real name was Shannon. Shannon Samuel. Go figure – as you can imagine how many fights in school that name got me. So I abbreviated it to just Non, which kind of works out fine. "You're going to stand outside and hand out these flyers. Make sure that you smile and ask them if they would like a flyer," he said handing me a pile of ill-stacked papers.

Can you believe that shit?! In New York City especially?! But I was naïve and wanted money so...

"Excuse me sir would you like to," I paused as the man just brushed pass as if he didn't know I was there. And this was basically what you'd get when you tried to handout flyers on a busy city corner. Folks in New York City didn't give a fuck about me politely asking if they wanted some flyer. Hell, I wouldn't. So imagine trying to stop a busy New Yorker and ask if he was interested in something he/she most likely care less about at the moment. It frustrated me though, for I never thought so many people could be so rude. I know. Where did I come from? Ha ha. But of course you learn things the hard way.

"Excuse me ma'am. Would? - Excuse me sir - Ex – Eh - Excuse," were the only words I could get out my mouth 98% of the time. Humiliation wasn't the word. I was just glad it was in midtown where I was less likely to see anyone of my peers.

I continued to do other things at the job like mop the floor, clean the restroom, and put up with all sorts of customer's attitudes and so forth. And when my first check finally came I was all excited about it. It was for $110 dollars. Hey it was my first check. So every Friday gave me another reason to continue. However, after a month of that shit-

"Man fuck this!" I yelled out in frustration, as I paced up and down the kitchen area of the back of the fast food joint. "You said I could leave at 10pm Khalid! And that's after you already made me stay an extra hour! Now it's 11:45 and you want me to wait another thirty minutes?! That won't do dukes."

"Look, no need for that," the manager Khalid snorted back. "I told you I'm waiting for the other guy to come in. And when he does," he paused for a moment holding two of his hands up as to motion me to calm down. "Then, you can go home. But until then, just hold tight."

I looked around for a moment pondering that notion, but then tossed it out. Perhaps had I not been so frustrated with having to work at the joint period. "Nah, I'm out man. No offense," I said quieting down as the other employees continued to look on. I just wanted to be out from that type of environment. You know… the minimum wage fast food hustle.

"Okay," said Khalid in a calm tone, quieting down as if in a relief himself, but as I headed for the door he continued again out loud for all the fast food joint to hear "Then bounce!! And don't think twice about showing your face!"

I was thinking twice alright, but it was not about showing my face at all. It was more like pondering on whether I should go back there and press his face against the grill. By this time I was embarrassed. It seemed like all eyes were on me waiting for a response.

"Man, fuck you! You wanna thump?!" was the only thing it seemed like I could reply with. He only smiled at me as if I was a joke, leaving me not only more embarrassed, but also feeling like a fool. As if that was the only clever thing I could come up with. I broke out mad.

'Who the fuck they think they playing?' I thought to myself as I stood a few steps outside the door. I felt incomplete. For some reason that whole scenario not only made me angry with the manager who played me in front of the patrons and coworkers, but they themselves as well. Was it because they were there to catch some form of entertainment from my humiliation? Go figure, but at that time in my life things like that bothered me. It made me think hard. It was nighttime now and equally cold as it was dark outside. So, there was nothing left for me to do but to continue down the dark cold streets of the big apple. I exited off 47th street to the F train.

From then I pursued other jobs, but they were all below mediocre. Let's see. I was a messenger, pizza delivery guy, bell-boy, valet… Man you name it. And the list goes on. Each job I left shortly just cause' I didn't have the tolerance level it took to deal with its' nature. The different customer attitude along with the peasant-like pay just wasn't working for me. Was I just spoiled? I mean most people tell you to be patient and that you have to start from somewhere. And don't get me wrong cause'

I was hearing them, but in the back of my mind I'm thinking to myself that this is not living. C'mon. If you've only got one life to live, why not live it to the fullest? I felt the urge to just do me and worry about the outcome later. These urges of course were on getting money the said 'easier way'. Hell everyone's fate is marked anyway. I was just tired of that petty living shit truly. I had nothing against making an honest living, but I wasn't about doing any backbreaking work for pennies either. Yeah I could count my blessings, but I preferred to count them faster. I wasn't asking to be rich. I just wanted to be able to live decent. And I wanted this. Now! But then, who was I kidding? What was I going to do? Sell drugs? Absolutely not. As much as the thought of that, along with the nothing to lose mentality was entertained, it all came down to my mother. Going off the said correct path would break her heart. See, she's all I had looking after me from the day I was born. I couldn't stand to see her struggle, but I didn't want to do anything that might increase the struggle on her behalf. So I continued with the menial jobs. So what if I was a mamma's boy? Ha ha.

"Hey ma", I said as I was coming home from another one of those hard workdays. The sounds of the famed calypsonian, Lord Kitchener filled the room. My mother always played her music when she wanted a peace of mind. Everyday that I came home from work I felt free from the frustrations of outside life. Yeah it was a shabby 2 bedroom apt, but it was home still. It was like a palace to me. Plus we had heat!

"Hey Shannon," she smiled back sitting at the kitchen table. "How was work today?"

"Just work. Doing this delivery crap. People just thinking they can walk all over ya cause you're the messenger type thing. The usual. I'll tell you ma. I'm tired." I pull up a seat at the table.

"You're tired," she says in a sarcastic tone as if talking to herself. "You barely started working. You dropped out of college telling me you're going to go back as if you expected me to believe that." Her voice elevated more and more in volume as she stared me down. She appeared to grow angry. It sounded so in her voice, but mixed with something else that would stick with me in the times to come. Disappointment. "What're you gonna do when you are my age?"

"Oh c'mon man!" I replied in great apparent annoyance as I threw up my hands. "Please don't gimmie that same speech. Can't you see I'm not trying to bust my ass till' I'm your age?! I-" I had to pause for I could see the tears welling up in her eyes. There was silence in the house for a few seconds that seemed like minutes. I then calmed back down and continued in a less assaulting tone. "I didn't mean it like that ma. You know I'm thankful for all that you endured for me. I-" There was a moment of pause again. What could I say? I already felt bad enough. And I always sucked at trying to make amends.

Then she broke the silence and continued softly. "I just wonder at times what are you going to do if something should happen to me? How will you cope? What will become of you?"

"C'mon ma. Why you?.." I paused to find better reasoning. "Why do you even think about things like that? You'll be fine. We'll be alright. Look, despite everything I'm still working. Ya know. Hanging in there" I felt that maybe she was just going through an emotional thing with the stress of everyday life. That she is known to worry too much. She's a worrier. But then she hit me with the words that up to this day is embedded in my mind, subconsciously replaying from time to time.

"I've been diagnosed with cancer," she calmly said looking down at the table as to hide her tears. "I... I had it for awhile and I.." she seemed to struggle to find the right way to finish. "I just did not want you to be scared"

Then with even more tears she faces me and says as if in pain, "You see why I want you to go back to school?" She then turned away again and stared out the window, just sitting in her chair.

It hurt me badly to see her cry. And coupled with this? I must've stood there looking at the ground for what seemed like forever. Then I went over and hugged her as if I hadn't seen her in years. And I just kept my arms around my mother trying to fight my tears. Trying to be strong. And I had the idea that I was never letting go. But you see, I had to let go. Not less than a year later she succumbed to the cancer.

***

So now I was on my own. I mean I had family members, but there were only a few I might consider turning to. Those that showed at the funeral gave their condolences and of course gave the traditional 'If there's anything you need' jargon.

"My condolences Shannon," said my uncle Charles. He was related to me on my father's side of the family. A said miser in his late 50's, or perhaps early 60's, and a wealthy one at that. "She was a real nice woman. If there's anything I can do just let me know. Your mother was like a close sister to me, so don't hesitate. Uhm," he stops and turns to his wife. I suppose to see if she was ready to leave.

She was a young one. 24 years old. Just 3 years older than me. My uncle Charles was apparent in age, but that never stopped him from charming his seemingly endless supply of women, young and old alike. I couldn't knock his hustle. And I took great comfort in his offer. The man did own a couple brownstones, in which his son whom was my age lived in one of them. So I figured if push came to shove that could be my ticket.

"Um, ok well take care," said Uncle Charles as he patted me on the back and exited out the church with his wife.

After receiving much sympathy from those who knew my mother well, I just sat in the pew and stared into space. The fact that Billie Holiday's 'come rain or shine' was playing brought me a little comfort and deep sorrow at the same time. I'm glad my mother could be sent off with that song, as it was one of her favorite. But then, it only brought back more memories of when she was alive. I wept to myself. And after the burial I knew that a part of me was gone forever.

Later on, back at my apartment there were a lot of people over just talking and reminiscing. I didn't feel like talking so I went in my room, shut the door and sat on the bed reminiscing to myself. Then there was a knock on the door. "I'm ok. Just in here resting," I replied to whomever was at the other end. Just to politely let em' know that I didn't want to be bothered. But then an all too familiar voice replied back from the other side.

"C'mon yout'. Let me talk to ya man" said the voice of none other than my cousin Trevor. Better known as simply..T.

"T!" I called out all too pleased as I quickly unlocked the door. "Whaddup my man?!" I asked as we exchanged the 'brothas' hug.

"Nothing much man. Just chillin" Then his face instantaneously grew more concerned. "Yo man. I'm. sorry man. Uhm. Yo, just get at me if there's anything I could do"

I only smiled back and looked down. Then I gave him a pat on the shoulder to assure him that his sympathy was much appreciated. I knew he felt the hurt too. That was his aunt. I knew he was sincere with what he said. He was like my brother. The only best friend I felt I could count on. That was my ace. We grew up together from childhood. But as we grew older we grew apart in distance. Yet, we remained good friends. Still close. He now resided in Jersey. He was a mellow fellow. Always pulling in the ladies cause' they dug his style. He smoked his marijuana religiously and rocked his braids in pride. A laid back kind of guy, just like yours truly. Yeah were like one and the same in most ways. In our persona you could call us twins, but in other than physical appearance, the similarities between us ended when it came to how he made a living. I always wondered about his Huck Finn life style. I mean he always worked off the books and seemed to have these underground connections from everything to firearms, to drugs, to banned books. He was one of those guys who were cool with all the folks who seemed to matter on the streets. And he seemed to be doing well for himself. I definitely could not knock his hustle. Long after, we talked and laughed about the good old times and then the apartment was once again empty. I just 'closed up shop' and went to bed, again thinking back. This led to a few more tears and then I consoled myself feeling that at least she didn't have to worry about me anymore. She must be in a better place.

As time went on I found myself more aggravated and short tempered, but I barely projected that out as much as I should have. The few minimum wage jobs I could get became more like a prison sentence. With every single pay I had only enough to maintain rent and...and that's it! Hell sometimes I had to ask or beg pardon from the landlady in IOU's. She knew my moms and me since I can remember and she often told me not to worry, but I still felt bad. I even tried working two jobs, but came to the conclusion that I was working all these hours, forever tired, and for what? Fucking folks on low decent pay still making more on some bullshit. The more this crossed my mind is the less tolerance I had for management. I must've just quit and quit until the few miniscule jobs I could get started to run out. I went three months without paying full rent before the landlady expressed her

concerns. I felt bad and packed my bags. I felt worthless.
I was going to now look for a shelter when I remembered
my uncle Charles. Feeling a little more hopeful I headed
for him.

Knock-knock. He came to the door after two
minutes. He seemed surprised to see me standing there
with my duffle case. "Hello Shannon," he greets to me
standing in the doorway. He looks down at my duffle bag
and then his facial expression changed just a little bit.
"What brings you?"

"Hey Uncle Charles" I replied admiring the silk
Japanese robe he donned. "Listen. I know it's late and
that this is on short notice, but-" I paused and looked away
already feeling bad. I could tell I was imposing. "I was
just wondering if I could stay here with you for a minute.
I just need to get straight." I babbled on about my situation
as he listened. Mind you we were by that time still in the
doorway. His reply?

"Let me talk it through with my wife", he replied
looking a little bothered. As if maybe I interrupted him
from his plush living or something. "Come inside and
um- wait a minute"

"Ok" I said. "Thanks uncl-"

"Hold on a sec" he interrupted as he headed up the
carpeted stairs. Was he annoyed? It seemed so, but I
didn't want to jump to conclusions. He was family and he
did offer his hand back at my mother's funeral. However,
the whole situation from the jump was looking kind of
grim. I just waited in the hallway, as he didn't really
invite me inside.

About 5 minutes later he came down with the
young wife. She too was wearing a silk robe, a matching
version to his. She too also looked annoyed. It was only
8:30pm. Did I wake them or something? "Well it's like
this," they both blurted out almost instantaneously. Then

the young lady nodded to Uncle Charles as for him to
continue.

"Things here right now are kind of tight. And
with the kids and all, well um, we just feel it's an issue of
space." He then paused. I guess to see if there was
anything I wished to add. But I only listened in
amusement. I already knew what was coming. He
continued, "I'll just be straight. It would put us at an
inconvenience."

Then the young wife added her piece. "I'm sorry.
It's nothing against you. It's just that it'd be kind of
awkward."

The thing is she didn't even look sincere when she
said it. She didn't even try to look sincere. But, who was
I to her? It was my uncle that got to me. I was hurt and
infuriated at the same time. I mean this was my uncle
man. And here it is he's just signing me off cause of some
bitch no older than me. Why all the 'if there's anything
you need' bullshit, if he really didn't mean it?! And he
knew my mother well. I wanted to yell this out to them,
but the only words that came out my mouth were.

"So uh… Not even just tonight?" I asked trying to
hide my disappointment.

Then the wife intervenes again sounding as
though more annoyed.

"Were you not listening? I mean this situation is
hard enough for us and-"

"Hard situation? You don't know the half" I cut
her off. Then I just looked at them in disbelief. I had to
tell myself to fuck it. What was the use of trying to draw
an understanding from them on my hard luck? "Tell you
what. Sorry I came. Don't sweat it," I said while picking
up my duffle bags. And with that, I left feeling nothing
more than anger in its' purest form. How dare they put
my face on the floor like that? Cold-shoulder me eh? I
had half a mind to go bash their heads together. Well then

all I had to feel to that was Fuck em. It's their house. I then made my way to the neighborhood shelter.

When I got there I stared up, and then just stared around. Did it really come down to this? This shelter I've passed over and over again from the time I was a child and never ever even imagined that I'd have to be claimed by it. Another bum. And that's what seemed to be all around me. Some of the same guys from that building were outside trying to squeegee folk's car windows for change. I just couldn't keep my head up as I entered the building. However, I quickly found myself back out when they told me that I needed to be on a waiting list.

"C'mon please ma'am." I began to stress. "I'll sleep in the doorway if I have to. I've just nowhere to go."

The response of the lady admin, whom was like the attendance gatekeeper for the shelter?

"So are the other folks on the list before you. So tell me what makes you so special?"

And although I guess she had a point, why did she have to say it like that? She was mean. I wasn't mean to her, but she seemed as though she got a kick out of messaging such burdens. I stared at her for a few seconds trying to figure out whether she just lacked people-person skills, or just truly enjoyed giving folks like me bad news. She looked back as if she wanted to say -"Well?!" she asked showing evident impatience.

Huh. She did say it. I looked over at the guard next to me. He was a considerably husky fellow. And he looked like he not only worked for the shelter, but was also a client. He only looked back with the same empty look as the desk lady. I left. I found shelter in an abandoned building not far off. It had some occupants too. But they didn't seem to pay me no mind. I made my way to an empty spot and pulled out a blanket I had in my suitcase. As I began to put myself at ease I started thinking of how my mother might roll over in her grave if she could see me now. I just started to reminisce over better times. And praying that this wasn't 'all that's wrote' for me. Surprisingly, it wasn't long before I was next on the list for the shelter. Just in time for Christmas. It was a relief.

***

All I could think about was taking a decent shower and a place to rest my head a little more comfortably. That whole month that I was on the streets I had to sneak into the YMCA every other day just to take showers. I mean suitcase and all. It was a marvel that I never got caught. I had a little money from pawning all the previous luxuries I had, like my radio, the television, etc. I got chicken scratch for what they were really worth, but who was in a position to be picky. But money, much like time for me, was running out. So I'm in the shelter now. A ghetto shelter at that. It was just like the abandoned building except for that it had working utilities. A mix of that along with some of the people ice-grilling you and you had an outdoor prison. Matter of fact, my first night there some dude tried to play me.

"Yo my man," says this huge fellow who looked like nothing more than a washed up thug. Let's just call him Baldhead. Cause' the guy looked like the black Mr. Clean. "My man, you can't lay there. That's my man's cot."

"Word?" I responded not wanting to get into anything, as I was already feeling stressed out. "Well, the lady gave me my stall number and all. This is it right here. Where's your man?"

Mind you that I was trying to sound as polite as possible.

"Yo fugg that shit! I said that's my man's cot," Baldhead repeated again, raising his voice as if he wanted to attract attention.

"Man be easy clown," I snap back. "I'll just go to the admin and tell em' to give me a new bed."

"Nah fuck that! The fuck you think you talkin' at you young punk muthafugga?!"

I pretended as if I was ignoring him and lay'd back down on the cot in a relaxed position with my hands folded behind my head. He continued to carry on.

"Yeah aiight muthafugga play deaf. Go to sleep tonight nigga and see if you don't wake up with a blade in your muthaphuggin chest!" he stated, still loudly.

"Yeah tell em!" somebody else yelled from the far row of the cot.

"Word up," the huge fellow continued as though growing more aggravated by my lack of response. "Muthafugga don't know who he fugging wit'"

And with that he went on and on for a minute. But I just continued to lye there without a word. That might have made me look as if I was soft or shook. Or even just the better man. But I was neither. He had already pissed me the fuck off and I was just pre-meditating my assault. I didn't care if he meant what he said. I will no longer allow anyone to play me. Fuck his size and his age. So a couple minutes after he calmed down I began to watch him out the corner of my eyes from time to time. He put on his headset, turned on his Walkman and laid down facing the opposite direction of me. Moments later he dozed off. When I felt he was asleep I went outside to get something to drink.

I brought a cola and a bottle of beer. The beer I guzzled down in the street and then stuffed its' empty bottle in my coat as a means to smuggle it. The cola I took sips of as I re-entered the building. When I got back to my cot I put the remainder of the soda pop on the make shift dresser-crate and sat back down on the cot. I then thought to myself if what I was about to do was necessary and if I really had anything to prove. But of course, he threatened me didn't he? So I took the empty bottle from out of my coat and approached him. He was sound asleep and looked so comfortable I almost hated to continue with what I was plotting.

"Aww, look at that" I mumbled to myself as I stood over his cot. His back still turned to me. I could almost see myself grinning through that shiny baldhead of his. I slowly crouched down so that I would be at the same level as him when he woke up. I started giving him a little nudge by his arms; like you'd do with a baby.

"Hey," I whispered. "Hey big guy. Wake up. Are you ok?"

He started to turn over slowly grumbling. "Hm? Wha..wha?" He moaned, trying to open his eyes from the deep sleep. When he finally did open his eyes and realize it was me, the next second and a half must've been the most alarming to him. His face looked a little panicked. I mean, what went through his mind in that instant? Ha ha. He must've been wondering in horror what the fuck was I doing over his bed. Ha ha again. Amusing.

"Hey buddy," I continued, grinning and talking in an ever so soft tone, as I didn't really want to wake anybody else up. "Remember me?"

His eyes widened and in that split second he tried to get up, I had already brought the empty beer bottle crashing down on his head. He screamed and grabbed his head where the blood was coming from. "Ahhh shit," he almost cried.

"Surprise star!" I jeered. "You're on stage fuck head. The spotlights on you."

"Ahh shit" he groaned again in agony, while holding his head with both hands and rolling back and forth in his cot.

"See what happens when you fuck with strangers?" I taunted. "It's the folks you don't know huh?"

By this time I was feeling cocky. I felt good knowing that I got my revenge. Now everybody in our section was up and watching. I just stood there as I watched him stumble off the bed, crawl to his crate and pull out a knife. He staggered up to his feet with his left hand still covering that wound. But now rage filled his eyes.

"Punk bitch," he grumbled. "I'm gonna tear you a new mouth."

"You see that?" I countered in amusement. "All those threats is what caused this in the first place. Are you telling me you wish seconds?"

I knew I'd have been more worried if not for the broken bottle I had in my hand. But just then, the security guard ambushed me from behind, shook-knocked the bottle from out of my hand and then just held me there in a choke hold.

"Hey man... Wha... What the fuck?!" I gasped alarmed, trying to break free as Baldhead lunged at me. I managed to twist halfway out from the guards grasp, but my assailant sank the blade into my side. Unbelievable pain. And the guard was still choking me. When he pulled the blade back out I knew he was going for my face next. In even more panic, I push-kicked him off with both legs and reached for the guards face, who was affecting an even tighter grip around my neck. I grabbed his ear and tried to pull it with all my might as he grunted in pain and threw me into the wall right by the doorway. I crawled towards the door and felt the sharpest pain in my leg. Baldhead had stabbed me in my right leg and then tried to jump on me as to hold me down. I rolled out of the way only to get grabbed by the security guard. He picked me up by the back of my shirt collar and slams me against the wall. I let him have a few punches, but it didn't seem to faze him much. He put both his hands around my neck and leaned me backwards over the banister. He was trying to push me over. He must've been trying to kill me. Just then Baldhead came over to me placing the knife to my neck.

"Please remember to say hi to all your relatives in the afterlife bitch." He says, pressing the knife to my throat.

And I could see it in his eyes. I was thinking to myself – so this is how it ends huh? Just when he looked like he was about to begin operation, some other guy grabs his arm. "Yo chill man. The admin called po-po" said the guy. His voice sounded familiar. It was the same voice that was cheering for Baldhead to kick my ass earlier. Baldhead attempted to cut me again, but the other guy insisted. "C'mon man! You ready to go back to prison again? Over this Nigga?"

This time Baldhead just stared at me. I stare back, but only my eyes are bulging cause' the other guard was still choking me. I didn't want to say anything that might provoke Baldhead to continue any further with that knife. After a couple of seconds of silence the guard loosened his grip. Then they backed up as if to allow me space to leave.

"Get the fuck out of here," the guard yells as if I was the one who had hemmed him up.

Boy would I've liked to give him his share of the bottle. I paused and looked back in the room where my stuff was in. They could see I wanted my things, but they stood there blocking the way with a look that dared me to make the attempt. All I could think of was the sentimental items I had in their of my mother. But to go back in there might've been suicide. I turned to make my way down the stairs. "I'll be back to get my…" I started to say as I took the first few steps down, but was cut short in sentence with such a heavy kick to my back sending me down the rest of the stairs. I woke up in the hospital.

I'm in some hospital in Brooklyn just mulling over some things. I thought about life in general. What was I going to do? I even thought about going back over to that shelter and putting myself into a '25 to Life' situation. But why? For them? Anyway, there was no

real reason to go back. The lady at the front desk
surprisingly sent my bag with me. And since I never got
the chance to unpack, what little I had was not left behind.

So now I'm just sitting there wondering about
what I was going to do next. I didn't want to do another
shelter. And fuck living in the streets. Nah. Damn that!
"Who do I have to...," I started to say to myself. And then
it hit me. I'll try my cousin Trevor! He was my last resort
at that point.

***

I called the next morning, but the phone just kept
ringing. So I decided what the hell. I'll just show up at
his door. And after I got there and knocked on the door
there were still no answer. So I just sat on the porch and
waited. I had to admire how quiet his neighborhood was.
"So this is how it is in Jersey," I said to myself as I eased
my back against the house, still admiring the serenity.

Dark came and still no T. I started to feel a little
sense of despair approaching. Just then, after 10pm I saw
his Sedan pull up to the drive way. He came out and when
he saw me he first looked alarmed and then relieved.

"Oh," he sighed in relief. "It's you. Don't do
them things kid. You almost gave me a heart attack."

"What? Who you're running from buoy'?" I
joked.

"I don't run buoy" he joked back. We always
joked around, trying to mimic the accents of our elders'
homeland now and then. He made his way up the stoop.
"Yo, C'mon inside," He motioned as he entered his house.
"How long you've been waiting here anyway?"

"Since 3:15." I replied sounding evidently tired.

"Since the noon?"

"Nah, since this morning," I answered
sarcastically.

"Don't get smart nigga. You're not inside yet"

23

"Ha. Nah man. You know how it gets. It's a sob story I have man. I'm about to right a book."

"Damn," he said, looking down. There was a brief pause and then he continued. "Well damn nigga don't just stand there. I mean you should've been inside. What? You don't want to come in?" he joked again to set the humor.

"Ok" I replied, grabbing my bag. "You don't have to tell me thrice'" And with that I followed him in.

23

Chapter II – My Boy Trevor

His house was very nice and roomy, I thought; for a guy his age. And Gottdamn it was warm. We sat at the table and I told him everything. At the end he looked frustrated. Then he asked. "Yo why didn't you just come here in the first place?"

"I don't know. I guess after my uncle shitted on me I just figured to hold off on that route a minute nah mean? I figured I'd just get in this shelter, find a start, grab my bearings and build. Hold my own. But..." I paused, almost overwhelmed with the frustration of the past ordeals with the more I thought of them. "..But even the simplest shit seems to be just too damn out of reach for the righteous."

"Yo man. Look. I hear what you're saying, but when I said if you need me I'm here. I meant that doggs."

"I know man. I know." I said, not knowing how to really respond. That was just one of the things I had to love about my cousin. He was always sincere. He always meant what he said and he had nothing but love for his folk.

"Yo. You can stay here man. I mean I got all this space. You know?"

"Yo... Yo man. I can't... I just can't thank you enough" I said, while trying to contain the overwhelming joy and relief that came over me.

"C'mon Man. You don't ever have to come at me on no humble shit. Nah mean?"

"I know man."

"Besides, when you get back up I can use some help with the utilities."

"Ha ha. That's a given"

That evening I settled in and we laughed about earlier times. That was the most unnerved I felt in a while.

Soon after, I got a temp job and then everything went smooth. I mean there were never any conflicts and that was really a peace of mind. Our schedules were different. I would do the usual 9 –5, or 12 – 3 or whatever the agency saw fit. T would seem to work seldom. Every so often he would run out throughout various time periods of the day usually in the evenings. Every now and then we'd hit a club or two. And that was it. It was just that after awhile I couldn't help but wonder what he was exactly into. I mean, nothing he had was too fancy-smancy, but for a guy our age he was doing quite well; that of an established, well aged man. He had a house in New Jersey, a pretty decent ride and always on top of the bills? In fact, there would be times he'd tell me not to worry about my half of the utilities. The kid just seemed to have his mind and his money right. I never bothered to ask cause' I figured it just wasn't my business. After all, although he's my ace and all, this was his place and I was thankful enough just to be here. But man, if I could just get right too; just so I could stand pon' me own two. Then I wouldn't have to feel like a burden. I wouldn't have to worry too much about the future. So one day I thought to myself, fuck it. We are boyz.

That evening Trevor came in with the grin that I knew all too well. He always had that grin when there was something exciting to let know.

"My youth," he almost taunted' as he came into the door and dropped onto the couch.

"Sup?" I asked.

"There's a bashment about to brew… Pool party and more poo'... Strictly on the excloo'... With these two broads who wants me…" he paused, handed me a flier on the event and then continued. "…And you - to be there." He eased back into his seat waiting for my response.

"Word?" I responded, examining the flier.

"Yes. Yes you will be there"

"Yes. Yes indeed I will be there. Ha ha," I humored back. "It says here that check-in started since 7o'clock this evening."

"And check out the check-out time."

"Sunday? A weekend bashment?"

"Yep. And I got the perfect ladies to roll with us for that occasion."

"Say word"

"Word Non."

"How much is all this?"

"The donation is like $500 a head. It's a popular bashment is why. But, that's not our concern cause' the girls insisted that they're paying."

"The women are paying?"

"Fuck. Why not? You know how much money I invested on these broads? It's only right they give a little now and then. Besides, they invited me. And in turn I invited you. We good bro."

"Yes we are," I cheered back. The more I thought about it the more I excited I grew. A weekend bashment, complete with pool party, floor party, drinks, room service and two beautiful women? And I knew they were beautiful just cause' T said so. He was always accurate on things like that. "We gotta hurry and pack then."

"No doubt. Quick time." He responded as he turned to enter the kitchen.

I just stood there for a moment pondering on the upcoming event. The more that I thought about a party of this nature the more I grew into a state of bliss. I mean yeah, to the average cat it would probably just be another party, but to me it meant more. I've never been to a party of that caliber in my short 22 years of life. I might've if I hadn't been hindered by despair, unemployment and homelessness. Here I was, not too long ago living on the streets, living in a shelter and worried that that might be my destiny. Only to be recovering from social exile into looking forward to the said 'Annual Party of Parties'. It was just one of many I would attend, but the idea of it the first time was a nostalgic feeling. Then my cousin Trevor came to mind. What would I have done if not for him? Where would I have gone? I had more appreciation for the guy, perhaps more than he ever knew. Nuff luv. And I marveled at how he held everything together still.

"Yo, what are you? How are you able to do all this?" I called out half jokingly to T, who was still in the kitchen, probably trying to fix a sandwich.

"Easy my youth. In time you may know the truth," he hollered back. Then he exited the kitchen with a mouth full of bread, an empty bottle of mayonnaise and muffles out with a full mouth, "Let's get packin."

***

It's now 10pm and we're cruising down the highway; Destination Fun. So what if we're a little late? No one goes to a party on time anyway. So we're in the car listening to the tunes. All is anticipation with me. Then I figured, now would be a good time to ask Trevor on what was his occupation.

"Yo, T" I began.

"Sup?" he asked.

"Just curious"

"Bout' what?"

"Uh… Yo, I was just curious man." I felt it hard to question a man on the way he might be making money. Not to mention my own suspicions.

"Bout' what muthaphucka?" he asked again, impatiently.

"Yo. Bust it. How you get down yo?"

"Cha' mean?"

"I mean. It's just that you seem to be doing well for yourself. Nah mean? And I was just curious as to how you apply yourself, cause' then maybe I can get down."

"Ah I see. You want to know how I do what I do."

"Yeah man. I mean what're you a lawyer? Street pharmacist? Porno-star? What?"

We both laughed. Then he answered. "Well I ain't one to hold nothing back. It's basically this. I sell guns."

"Guns?" I asked. "You got all this dough from selling Guns?"

"Well I ain't exactly rich Nigga" he humored.

"I know. But I'm saying, just guns?"

"Yeah. I got my own little clientele on the side" he replied, as he began to check for another radio station due to the growing bad reception from being too far from town. After he settled on a clearer station, he eased his driver's side seat back a few notches and continued, "They know I got what they want. They trust my shit. They aint gotta worry about it being used, or having bodies or nunna' that. Plus, my shit is cheap."

"Ha. You sound like a fucking used car salesman" I joke.

"Ha ha" he laughed.

Then afterwards we just continued down the road in silence. I rolled over what T was talking about in my head for most of that night. I figured that would be rather an exciting thing. And with that, heck, maybe I could get 'right' after all. So I pushed the envelope a bit.

"So uh... There's anyway you think I can get down?" I asked.

"You wanna be down buoy?" he asked in a joke mock manner.

"Very funny."

He stared for a few seconds as if trying to calculate his decision. And then he responded. "Alright, Fuck it. You can get down. Next run I go on I'll let you come through."

"Ok. Bet," I replied. But I was still thinking that there had to be more to it than that. And in time I found I was right. Man was I right.

When we finally got to the mansion it was 11:30pm. There was a big banner in front that read 'Ballahz Ballroom Ball 99'. It was indeed an eloquent looking peace of work; your typical expensive Palace type joint. The women T was talking about had already checked in. Then T suggested that we just dump the bags in the room and explore around. As we took the tour of the happenings at the hotel I noticed that it was the scene of ghetto luxury. The giant pool was filled with women in their thong-ta-thong-thong-thongs. There were folks on the basketball, tennis and handball courts in the back, complete with perfect lighting for playing at night. People were doing nighttime BBQ on the concrete grills that was built in near the court. Folks were socializing at the bars that occupied a couple rooms. There were the main party floors; one & two, which were named just that. Chromed out everything! And enough rooms to actually accommodate the crowds. There were picture frames all over the main hall depicting the founder and his close relatives. It appeared to be black owned. The party ratio for the night, however, was a good mix. Not bad. It became apparent that the owner(s) of this mansion styled abode had a good business sense in mind when developing this atmosphere. Lease or rent it out for functions. It was like your rich uncle's house or something. A pretty good money making deal. And with the crowds of people that would show up there, I'm sure a healthy amount of funds were endlessly coming in. Figure at least 200 people are here tonight. Just 200, which in tonight's case, is a very modest number and you figure that's $100,000. Jeez. I was impressed. But enough money talk. The party was jumping.

"Yo cuz," I yelled out to T. "What you wanna do first?"

"Her," he replied, pointing towards one of the two ladies, whom were both approaching. They looked fine as hell. They also looked expensive. PRODA up and down. "Non. These are the two lovely ladies I was telling you about. Ladies, this is my cousin Non."

"Hi Non. It's nice to meet you," one lady replied. Then she focused her attention back to T. "You didn't tell me your cousin was so handsome." She turned back and gave me a fine smile.

"I shouldn't have to. We're family. Can't you tell the resemblance?" he answer back with a Cheshire cat grin. "So uh. Ladies. What is on the agenda for tonight?"

"I don't know. But uh, I hope you didn't plan on hanging with us tonight?" she replied.

"What?" said T, maintaining his grin. "Y'all better stop playing around."

Then the other girl intervened. "Who's playing? We already paid for your ass to get in. Uh... No. There's too much going on over here for us to be tied down with you."

"Ahh. You're gonna play off my game in front of my cousin?" asked T humorously in his normal cool composure. "Yeah alright. Well all is fair ladies. Just save me a dance."

"Aight T. Just join us in the pool later," said one of the ladies. "And bring your cute cousin," they said, as they exited back into the party.

"Damn T. Them some fine ladies there," I commented as we stared at the both of them making their way onto the dance floor. "We chillin' with them tonight?"

"The Tina sisters?" he replied as he picked up a drink, still trying to get a glance at them from the crowd. "Nah, them my girls. I knew them since I came out to Jersey. They both soon to take over their folks family business is why they so loaded though. We play around and what not. We cool. That's why they paid for our tickets. We look out for each other now and then. I'm like their teddy bear body guard."

"They fine as hell T."

"Think I don't know? I think one of them digging you."

"Which one?"

"The quiet one. Carla. You didn't see how she was looking?"

"A little bit."

"Well you should've said something doggs?"

"In time cousin. Don't sleep on my skills. I just play the silent role a bit. Get the feel of a situation, ya know. That's just how I do."

"Whateva Nigga. We gonna have to get you out of that shy role."

"Don't play me," I joked back.

"Let's check this party man."

And so we did. It seemed like a formal/informal affair. I say that because you had dudes there with tuxedos, but then you also had guys there with jeans and leather jackets. It was as if there were 2 separate fliers handed out – each with their own dress code. A combination I wasn't all too familiar with, but nonetheless a righteous party. The year 00' was right around the corner and the mood was a festive one. T went to mingle with some guys he recognized for a sec, leaving me to wander the scene for dolo. I just figured that it left more ladies for me. I would just play the bar scene.

"What'll it be chief?" asked the bartender.

I wasn't no connoisseur of alcoholic substances so I just replied with the drink that seemed to be all the craze' at the time. "Cognac," I replied trying to sound like I was a regular.

"We outta Cognac."

"Ok. Um. Gin & Juice."

"You got it."

"Thanks sir," I replied as I took the drink and leaned back against the bar counter. I was just there chillin', taking in the sights and admiring the view. Just then I look across the bar and there is this unbelievable fine sistah just giving me the eye. I'm thinking - Me? Nah. I turned around and took a few sips of my drink. I glanced back and she was smiling, almost as if she knew me. So I smiled back. I made a motion with my hand communicating the question to her if it was ok for me to come over and she gave me the ok nod.

"Hi," I said, while trying not to grin to hard.

"How're you doing?" she asked with the smile that would stay on my mind for weeks.

"Chillin," I replied still trying to keep the composure. Whatever I was drinking was making me get too comfortable. I mean to the point I would forget myself comfortable. And she was bad'. I mean she was honey golden brown, thick and curvaceous in all of the right places, cute face and all. And her eyes – Gottdamn! Her eyes were the type that'd always make you look down or away if you tried to stare into them too long.

"You came with T right?" she asked.

"Yeah. That's my bro."

"Oh, you're brothers?"

"Nah, not my brother brother, but he's like my brother. Ya know? I mean we're related. We're cousins." I answered, yet fully aware that I was beginning to babble. That's a common symptom when you catch PWS-'Pretty Woman Syndrome'. It happened to a lot of guys when they try to hold their composure and sound cool in front of a 'too pretty' lady. I took another sip of my drink and again reminded myself to be cool. Let's get it together, for their aint' no duck niggas over here. She's a nice young lady and this can be done. I had to play that in my head a few times.

She continued. "Cousin huh? So I see Trevor was right when he said handsome men run in his family."

"Oh," I chuckled to myself. "T said that huh?" she only smiled back. "Well I'm sure sorry T never told me about you because…" Just then I paused in conversation when this taller husky fellow came up behind her. He iced-grilled me for a second and then turned to her.

"Fuck is this?" he starts. "I turn around a few seconds and you over here flirting with some duck nigga?"

"Duck nigga?!" I answered back.

Right after, the lady cuts back to the meathead. "First of all I ain't your woman so don't even come at me like that. Second…"

"Fuck that," the husky rowdy fellah interrupted. "You came with me up here so you're my woman tonight! Aight?! Everything was and still is on me. Aight?! So don't get it twisted, or I promise you can find your way home."

By this time I could sense that she was getting embarrassed. And although the majority of the floor was into their own worlds dancing, he was still loud enough to turn a couple heads around the bar. So I felt it my duty to intervene.

"Aye man," I began to try to reason with the aggressor. "Look. It's my fault. Aight? I tried to step to her and she wasn't even feeling me. She was just being polite that's all." There. I felt I had said my peace.

Then she intervened again. "You don't even have to make any excuses on my behalf mister. He's not…"

"Yo shut up. Shut the fuck up and let the man finish," he interrupted even louder than before, drawing more attention. "I want to hear what the man has to say." He then turned back, looking down his nose towards me. "Go head duke. Say sumptin." He almost seemed to dare. Actually, he was.

We're now staring eye to eye as he approached closer. This time even a few more heads start to notice.

They could tell by the way he was stepping to me that something was about to go down. After ice-grilling each other for a few seconds I start to talk.

"Well, I was going to apologize, but since you want to play gorilla..." I paused to inch up closer and let him know where I was coming from.

At just that moment, T shows up out of nowhere. "Whoa," he said coming in between and pulling me back. Then he faced the knucklehead whom I was about to let have it. "Yo, easy Grip. Relax. That's my family."

"Yo, this your cuz T?" the guy Grip asks.

"Yeah man. We gotta run outside on some biz real quick. Alright?" He asked, looking as though he was waiting for some approval.

"Believe me T. Only cause' it's you." He then turned back to me while supposedly still talking to T, but really referring to me. "You got to tell your cousin to be more careful. It's too dangerous out here to just go stepping to just anyone."

Then he let out a few chuckles as he exited the bar with a crew of guys whom I didn't even know were there with him. They just seemed to appear out of nowhere. And T? I never heard my cousin plea bargain with anyone like that. The hell was that guy? T turns with me to go out the other exit. Now we're outside.

"The fuck we're doing outside?" I start. I was still highly upset about what had just gone down. See, all I could remember was some guy trying to play me in front of the crowd. "That clown in there just tried to play me on some bullshit!"

"Ah don't try to get hype about it now." Replied T.

"What? What're you trying to say?"

"Well look, first things first. What happened in there?"

"Nothing much man." I replied, still a bit frustrated by the statement T made about me not doing anything at the bar. Hell, had he not stepped in he don't know what might've went down. But, the guy did bark on me. That's what the few that were standing there saw. That's what was bothering me. Why should it have though? I guess that I was a more hotheaded fellah at the time. "Dudes lady comes up to me and he gets jealous. He tried to get fly."

"And you tried to get fly back."

"Well nah. Not off the jump. I just tried to smooth things out with him and his lady."

"Why?"

"Cause he was embarrassing her."

"But still. Why?"

I paused for a moment actually trying to remember why myself. Then it came back to me as I replied, "What the fuck is this a pop quiz? Cause' dukes tried to play me. He called me a duck and all that shit. Talking all that shit as if I wasn't in the room."

"Is that it? You sure it wasn't just that you felt the girl was fly and you wanted to play the chivalrous muthaphucka?"

"What?" I began to feel myself grow more frustrated with him. It almost sounded as though he was defending that other clown's position. "Nah. As a matter of fact, it was because she was there that I didn't just stall on his ass. And why the fuck are you coming at me as if you're trying to find fault with my case in the matter? I mean, who is this Nigga and why the fuck are we still talking about this? I'm only growing more frustrated. I'm liable to go back and…"

"And do what?" he interrupted. "Son, do you even know what he is?"

"Fuck what he is. Fuck what he is and do he know what I am" I stated back in bold.

"Just relax a minute Non. Let me explain something to you…"

"Uhum, I'm listening" I interrupted mockingly.

"Good. Well then listen," he starts to put his hands up as to let me know to cool it. "That guy whose ass you were so getting ready to bust – is a representative for an Organization – you…"

"Organization? So what the fuck does that mean? He's a door-to-door business man?" I humored. I all of a sudden felt that the whole thing was ridiculous and was already beginning to calm down. I just wanted to make light of the situation.

However, T, he wasn't laughing. He just continued, "No. More like a door-to-door hitter."

"Hitman?! What are you… Are you kidding me?"

"No. Matter of fact, those guys he walked out with, they're shottas too. They all work for him."

"You don't say," I responded a little amused. There was a brief pause as he searched my face for a response. "Wow. I um… I…"

"Yeah. You seem to realize now that…"

"I don't give a flying fuck if he was the shitman" I interrupted. "Am I supposed to be scared?" T only looked at me in amusement. There was a brief pause again. Then he started to laugh. The situation was kind of funny so I laughed too. "What the fuck are we doing out here anyway T? What're you trying to tell me? And what the hell are you doing associating with a bunch of men like that? Are you a hitman too?" I humored.

"Ok. Fuck it," he answered still laughing. "I guess I was just trying to get your response to the matter."

"Yeah, you think I'm a punk my yout'. You don't know man. I throw down."

"Yeah alright. Alright," he said, as we regained our cool. "But serious though Non. I'm sure you one bad dude. Aight?" he humored.

"Word up," I responded, mock-confirming that notion.

"But Non, still," he said as he placed one hand on my shoulder. "I know this guy. He's a killer and he's an unreasonable one at that. I don't want any problems. All's I'm saying is just avoid him tonight, cause' if you meet up again he might try to fuck with you again. Non. He's a very sadistic muthaphucka. You would think he's playing and all is well and then the next thing you know, you're dead. And Non, if something were to happen to you, you know it's family first. I don't have to tell you I might end up in the papers. Lay low awhile. Besides, he's only here for one night."

"Damn. It's like that huh?" I took a pause as I turned around and pondered this whole ordeal. I didn't give a fuck really, but if T was saying he didn't want any problems then so be it. I didn't know what kind of relationship T had with these fellows and I didn't want to compromise our lives. So I figured I would lay low and retire to my room for tonight. "Well T, you know I don't go for muthaphuckas trying to play Da' Gooch on me, but sure, I'll stay out the way."

"Aight Non," said T, as he patted me on the back"

"So tell me something," I began as we made our way back to the mansion.

"What's that?"

"What the fuck will you be doing?"

"Me? I'll be at the party?"

"Say what?"

"Yeah dukes. You're the one that has to lay low. Not me."

"Alright T. Alright," I waved off as I made my way up the stairs.

"Yo Non. Don't look it at that way man."

"Sure," I replied as I turned out of sight. I couldn't believe that I was allowing this Grip fellow to give me a curfew. I mean, cause' that's what it basically came down to. Well fuck it. I did feel kind of relieved that we were no longer bickering about some smuck who thought he was badder than bad. Yeah, the fact that he was supposed to be some hitman, or a representative of, or whatever the fuck his title did catch me a bit on the cautious. Maybe this was best.

The next morning, I woke up, got showered and dressed; and headed for the lobby to the commotion of bewildered faces, EMT's and police officers. "What's going on?" I asked one of the spectators.

"I think somebody got shot outside of the parking lot," replied the on looker.

"Kidding me," I mumbled to myself. I started to walk around slowly, excusing myself past the crowds. All I saw was that they zipped up some unfortunate soul in a body bag and loaded the remains in an OCME truck. It was unreal. I had to find T. I searched up and down the place, but didn't find him. Then I got the uneasy thought that what if he was the victim, but as I rushed back to my room there he was.

"T," I began

"Yo Non. I was looking for you."

"T, what happened man?"

"I don't know. I woke up a little early before you to get breakfast at the diner. Next thing you know some girl screams out in the lot and comes in with a bunch of frantic guys. At first I thought she was screaming for help from them, but then they all were screaming 'call the ambulance-call the police!'"

"Damn," I said, as I eased down in the chair. "You say in the parking lot? Weren't we just out there last night? Shit." There was a pause as I tried to let everything sink in. Who knows when this thing happened? Then I remembered last night's ordeal again. Could this have had anything to do with those supposed dangerous individuals I almost had the physical confrontation with? "Yo T."

"Sup?"

"You don't suppose this had anything to do with that knucklehead at the party last night do you?"

"Interesting thought."

"Do you suppose that they're still here?"

"I'm not sure."

"Hm," I pondered to myself. Then I started to look at T. I remembered that he seemed to know those guys well. Not to mention that he didn't seem to feel bothered in the slightest. Like, why was he so eager for me to retire to my room last night really? I mean, all of a sudden these hit-guys are mentioned and someone is dead in the parking lot? But maybe I was just jumping to conclusions. Who's to say that it was them? Who's to even say that it wasn't just some yahoo with a gun who got a little bloodthirsty in an argument or something? I entertained the thought for only a minute, but then figured it wasn't really my job to solve murder cases. So I headed for the bathroom to take a wiz.

Just then, T made a statement that I find funny only now, yet shook me a bit at the time.

"But if it did have anything to do with those knuckleheads in the bar last night, then I'd say you'd be a pretty lucky guy. Don't ya think?"

I peered back out the bathroom and looked at T. "Yeah, I suppose. I suppose so." He only had that smirk on his face that he'd have sometimes when he was trying to humor a situation. And although there was nothing humorous about it, I played it off with a chuckle. Soon we were back in Jersey and I was back to work.

***

"Non!" starts my jerk faced boss. "Why are you late?"

"I'm sorry. It was the train."

"Well had you got up earlier then you wouldn't have to worry about the train would you?"

"I guess not."

"So don't let it happen again," he snorted as he turned to walk off.

Now I suppose I could have just let that slide, being that he was my boss and all. But it bothered me that this man thought he could talk to me like that. And I kept wondering if it was a race issue, because I was the only other black guy, who was usually on time in that office; compared to a few of the other guys who were late countless times, new and old employees alike. And to top that off, I also noticed how naturally he'd seem more comfortable around his own kind than Theo and I, who happened to be the only two black guys in our dept. When he dealt with them he was all smiles and understanding. When it came to us two, who purposely never goofed off mind you, he'd always talk serious and firm with a cold stare and tone that read, 'you must know I don't like you, but you know – affirmative action. Like he'd always seem like he was preparing himself for us to jump him or something. Heck, Theo was a quiet dude, so he'd just go on as if nothing bothered him. But it bothered me; A lot. I mean, you don't have to like me, but now you wanna' play me too? So I stepped to him as he was walking towards the hall.

"Hey Mr. Killough," I began.

"Yes. What is it?" he turned around, still eyeing some paperwork he had in his hands.

"Help me to understand. Did you just say the words, 'Don't let it happen again' to me?"

His attention immediately shifted from the documents he had in his hand to me. "Yes I did. Why? Does that bother you?"

"Well it just depends on who says it Mr. Killough. For example, my parents could get away with that, but when someone else out of my family tells me that, especially a man like you, I get really bothered," I answered with a stern face.

"Really. Well what exactly is a man like me, Mr. Samuel?"

"Do I have to say it, Mr. Killough? A racist, a bigot, prejudiced, whichever you prefer."

"Oh. So now you think I'm a racist. Why? Is it because I won't allow you to get away with all the jive you want to pull?"

"First of all Killough…"

"Mr. Killough," he interrupted.

"Killough…" I continue in defiance. "You're beginning to piss me off. And you don't want to do that. You know damn well I don't fu..." I catch myself from the dirty slang. "..You know I don't play around in here. Second, I'm not Theo. Now, I know I'm a temp and that it only takes a phone call to get me out of here, but let's get one thing straight. Be it you're a racist-bigot, or just an asshole towards non-whites, or whatever you want to call it, you will not play me," I stated clearly as I kept my calm, yet frustrated tone.

He looked surprised. And he should've. The fuck he think this was, a movie? He said nothing as he turned around with a smirk on his face and continued to his office. From there I expected to get relieved of my assignment, but nothing. I waited until the end of the day, but still nothing. After 3 weeks, I had forgotten that the whole thing happened. Until, the agency called.

"Mr. Samuel please," requested the agency rep on the phone line.

"This is me."

"This is Ned from the agency. I'm going to have to end your assignment."

"You don't say," I responded trying not to sound too surprised. "How come?"

"The client, Mr. Killough, claims that you used his credit card and ordered something out of a catalog."

"What?!" I now began to really sound surprised. "The fuc... Ordered what?!"

"A desk lamp or something like that. It doesn't matter. The point is he's claiming that he believes you used his credit card that he had left on his desk."

"But I didn't! He's just trying to get back at me over some misunderstanding a few weeks back. He didn't tell you?!"

"Misunderstanding? No, he did not. Well, he said that he wouldn't press any charges cause' he didn't feel it was important enough to do so."

I interrupt in frustration. "Are you listening to me? Why the fuck would I want to use his credit card to order a fucking desk lamp? That doesn't make sense!"

"Well you said there was a misunderstanding between you two. Perhaps the order was made in bad blood."

"What?"

"Well look. He's a very important client to us and we can't risk jeopardizing that. So we can't send you back there."

"Ugh. I can't believe this sh… Oh ok. Well look, just put me on another assignment."

"I'm afraid we can't do that."

"Ugh again. Here we go. Why not Ned?" I asked sarcastically.

"Well it's just that Mr. Killough has been one of our clients for years and he just doesn't seem to have a reason to lie."

"So you believe him," I stated out, more so than a question.

"Well it doesn't matter what we believe, but your behavior during this brief conversation didn't help your case much either. I'm sorry. You understand."

"Oh really," I responded now enraged. "I understand Ned. I mean, why would I sound frustrated when I'm being accused by a bigot and an equally guilty plastic agency?"

"That's a serious accusation Mr. Samuel."

"Oh yeah I understand. I understand that you've probably only tolerated this little conversation as long you had to, because you probably get a kick out of it. Or maybe you're waiting for me to make a death threat to add more pain to humiliation. Huh? What is he paying you, you fuck?"

"Of course he's paying us Mr. Samuel," he interrupted in a nonchalant tone. "That's how we make our money. He is a client."

"—You MOCKING me!?" I began to yell out on the phone in deep anger. "—FUCK you and your agency you GOTTDAMNED DICK HEA...!"

"Click," the rep hanged up, leaving me on the other end to hear the dial tone. And at that moment, I wanted to kill everything about that agency that I felt brought me unneeded frustration. I was just in a silent psychotic rage, standing still by the phone. Then I calmed down. Could I really get mad at the agency? They were just looking out for their own interest, which seemed to be a common trait amongst traditional bloodsucking corporations in this city. Nah. It was Mr. Killough who had to get his. He just had to get his somehow. I tried to sleep it off, but I couldn't get past that arrogant George Bush Jr. smile.

The next thing I knew is that I was approaching cousin Trevor on an unexpected topic.

"T," I began to ask as we're sitting down in the room watching the Nature Channel.

"Sup?" he asked, while concentrating on a television program. "I love this channel. It's madd calming."

"Nah, not that."

"Sup?"

"I want to buy a piece."

"Could you be talking about a gun?" he joked sarcastically. His attention still not diverted from the program on T.V.

"I'm straight up. I'm going to kill my former boss."

"What?" He had a surprised look of amusement on his face as he turned to face me.

"Yeah. And I'm only telling you, cause' I know you won't say nothing."

"What? Is this over the job incident?"

"Yeah."

"Aww. You don't want to risk throwing your life away over no job do you? Like them white boys?"

"Well it ain't about being white. Besides, they go in and kill everybody cause' they lost their job. I just want to kill Mr. Killough because he tried to play me."

"Oh yeah? How's that?" he asked, as he started to lean forward in interest.

"It's the principle. He lied on me. He lied on me on some bullshit. What if I was supporting a family and needed that job? Or going through a crisis like I was before I came here? He didn't think about that. Nah. I did all my work without goofing off and he just decided to lie on me, cause' he's a bigot-jackass. As far as I'm concerned, when he did that, he basically said - Ha-Ha. He's basically like – Fuck what you're going through, cause' I don't like you anyway. Nah mean?"

"I see. The last laugh," he replied still with the amused expression.

It was as if he wanted to laugh. I could feel that he might be mocking me, but I continued anyway.

"Word up. That shit just drives me to the dark end." I paused to search T's expression again on the matter. He was just nodding in agreement wearing a silly smirk on his face. I thought to myself, enough is enough. Is he going to help me or was he just being entertained by my aggravation too? "T. Are you laughing at me man?" I asked in annoyance.

"Nah man, I just had a thought. You definitely seem to have the will, but for the wrong type of shit," he replied.

"What?"

"You get mad and you start bringing up all sorts of issues to psyche yourself up to the moment. That shit about the 'What ifs I was down and out' don't matter. You just think too much."

"Wha...? I don't get where you're..."

"See here. I think you'll be alright in this thing Non."

"T. What the fuck is you talking about man? Are we even on the same topic?"

"I'm talking about putting you down cousin. I'm talking about putting you down with the operation. You were interested weren't you? Are you still?"

"Well uh… sure. Definitely."

"Ok. I've got a run coming up tomorrow night. You can witness how things go down, while picking up some pointers as we go."

"Yeah T," I responded more calmly, yet somewhat surprised.

"Tomorrow then," he confirmed as he shifted his attention back to the TV, in which there were a scene showing a pack of wild bobcats tearing apart the remains of a deer. "This situation can always hold my interest yo," he stated, referring to the graphic scene that just took place on the program. Or was he?

I was in a daze like situation the rest of that night. Was it that easy? Finally, was this it? I remember fantasizing about finally standing ground on my own two. I thought that from then, I could start planning ahead for my own future. When I think about it now, maybe I was just too naïve. But see, ever since before my mother died I felt it was so important to find a niche and make things happen for us. Now she's gone and I never got the chance. I felt that if T kept his word, which he was usually always good for, then this could be my ticket towards redemption. Only at the time, I don't think I really understood what I was trying to redeem myself from. I'm still not too sure. Anyhow, T did keep his word, for the next night we went on the road trip. I just wasn't prepared for what came next.

Chapter III – An introduction to 'WTF?!'

"This is it," T said, breaking the 1½ hour silence.
"It looks like dismal."

"Yeah. It's an old abandoned ship yard."

"Hm."

"Wait here a sec Non. I'm going to check to see if everything is cool."

"No doubt," I quietly said to myself.

He disappeared into some shabby old looking warehouse. The place all around looked like a scene out of Scooby Doo; Creepy. I felt very uneasy parked in this wide-spaced vacant lot. Almost nothing seemed visible in the pitched-black night. So I just sat there with the seat leaned back keeping silent. I dunno. Maybe I was afraid something was going to grab me through the car window if I made any type of sound. One too many horror movies. Then T seemed to have materialized from out of nowhere leaning right next to my side of the window.

"Shit!" I sat up startled.

"Ha-Ha," he laughed. "Spooky looking area huh?"

"Don't do that T man," I had to let out a little relieved laugh.

"C'mon yo. We gotta go inside."

"Ok. Cool with me."

As we made our way into the building I was beyond surprised. There, in that building was the same jerk-off that I had the altercation with at the Ballaz Ballroom', along with 4 other guys. They all looked at me grimly. At first, the thought that I was setup had crossed my mind, but that notion quickly perished, as I knew that T wouldn't ever deal in such an atrocity. We were like blood. The idea also went away when I noticed a gagged, blindfolded and bound man lying on the floor. When T and I came closer I could see that he was a middle-aged looking black man. He was still alive and just lying there. Probably he knew already what might've awaited him.

Then Grip, apparently the ringleader, broke the silence. "Welcome tough guy," he said with a grin on his face. The same sadistic grin he gave me in the bar that night when he suggested to T I be more careful. I could never forget that grin. Especially in light of what happened the following day. "Tonight is your night."

"What?" I replied, sounding just a little less sure of myself than from our last confrontation.

Then his facial expression began to change back to a serious stare. "You mean, you don't even know why you're here?" he asked, sounding a bit amused.

I looked around and there's all these guys just ice-grilling me. I looked over at T who only glared back with a more concerned look. I only let out a shrug and answered with a wild guess. "We're here... Uh... For this guy. Right?" It was the best I could do.

He only let out a laugh as T stepped in.

"Grip! What the fuck? Why this? Why him now in this case?" T asked, sounding frustrated and pointing to the gagged man lying on the floor.

"Yo! I already told you. This – is how it has to be. – IF HE WANTS IN!" Grip began to shout suddenly.

"Yo. Don't FUCKING yell at me!" T shouted back in retaliation.

"Hey easy," said one of the guys calmly in the background shadows. "Take it easy. Let's get back to the matter at hand."

"Hey shut da fuck up you," Grip replied to the voice in the background. "This is my show. And right now, I'm about to cut all this bullshit and hand the spotlight over to my man Non over here."

Now how the fuck did he know my name is what I remembered concerned me for a little while after that. But when he pulled a pistol from out the inside of his leather-bomber jacket, how he knew my name was the least of my concern.

Then I started to smile as I thought to myself that this whole thing might've been a prank T was trying to pull. Maybe we were just meeting up with these guys in their clubhouse or something on the way to pick up the guns and T thought it would be a good idea to mess with my head on the way. It was the only thought that brought me some comfort at the time so I started to smile a bit in comfort. That is, until Grip went on again.

"Oh. You think this is funny huh?" said Grip, as he approached me with the pistol in his hand.

So long for the comfort. I recall even wanting to run, but I maintained my ground. He got in front of me and stared down with smoking eyes, exactly like when we almost had the showdown at the bar. And then at that moment, I remembered growing my balls back.

"What would you have me do?" I asked. Though I already knew the answer.

Grip handed me the pistol and pointed to the man on the floor. Then he stepped back into the shadows with the others. I slowly stepped over to the man on the ground. He stuck his head up and looked around, I suppose trying to figure out exactly where I might be positioned.

"It's already cocked and loaded for you big boy. All you have to do is pull the trigger," I heard Grips voice echo from the background. "He's just a dirty no good informant."

I stood over the blindfolded man and just stared down. He seemed to be trying to muffle out a couple words. I felt woozy. This couldn't be happening. All I wanted to do was get down with what T was doing? And this was it? I no longer felt as if I wanted any parts. I wanted to back down. I felt I was on the verge of backing down. I just stood over the subdued helpless man and stared. My mind was somewhere else.

Then I was brought back when someone tapped me on the shoulder. It was T. He spoke quietly so that only I could hear. "Under no circumstances did I want it to go down like this, but Non, I just have to let you know that it would be in your best interest to go ahead with this. Don't worry. I'm here." He then backed off into the shadows.

Like that made me feel any better. Of course this was something I just didn't want to go through. I mean, what the fuck was this? Who were these guys really? And why the hell did I have to do their dirty work? And to make matters worse, an alleged informant. A fucking man I didn't even know and he was just lying there. He couldn't see or speak, but he was very much alert and could hear. The whole matter had me highly upset. He began to look tense as though he couldn't take the wait any longer. No, I really didn't want to do this. But after what T told me, I knew that if I didn't do him I would get done in myself. At least that's the impression I was under at the time. So I aimed the gun directly at the man's chest. I was sweating a bit now and was trying to convince myself to pull the trigger.

Then Grips voice alerted me again from the shadows. "Non. What the fuck? It's already cocked so just pull the trigger. There's no thinking involved in this. Just do it," he ordered as I just nodded in agreement and took a step closer to the guy, still aiming the gun at him.

"I got it," I replied.

"Oh you do?" he mocked. "Then aim for the head."

The man started to breathe hard and braced himself, as I was steady aiming – pausing – about to squeeze – just about to squeeze. The gagged soul then started to let out muffled screams.

"Look fellas..." I began.

"No, you Look!" interrupted Grips voice, yet again from the background, like a constant blasted devil on my shoulder. "You see that there? He's daring you! And not only that, he's an informant! A threat to this thing we have here. Do him or get done!"

"Ok." I replied, now with both hands leveling the gun as to ease the strain that was coming on to my right arm. In my mind, I was trying to justify this impending deed with the threat that was just directed towards me, as a source to gain the momentum needed.

Grip continued, "This is your chance to be apart of something greater than you've ever been through in your whole mediocre existence. You get this ticket cause of T. So do not fuck up your first job."

With that he disappeared back into the shadows. And with that I also knew it was my final warning. He didn't just reveal all of this to give me a simple lecture. I wasn't here to witness all of this and still be entitled to an option. This was more like – you're here, you know, you 'do' or there is nothing left for you beyond this point. It was plain and simple. And quite frankly, being left with that reality, it made everything just that clearer for me.

The man's faced turned dull as I approached him again, this time with the sure intent to pull the trigger. I felt that I had already got on Grip and the crew's unsure side just by taking too long and having Grip explain it to me. I'm not sure where it came from, but something in me told me that if I had to do something like this, then what did it matter at this point? He was dead anyway. I didn't know the guy, so fuck him. On a twisted psychological impulse, I knelt down next to the man and layed the gun on the ground behind me. I did un-gag the man. I felt that if I had to do this guy, he shouldn't be totally helpless. Go figure; that didn't help much.

"You don't have to do this," the wounded subject at first tried to reason, as I stood back up and re-leveled the gun. But then, as if he finally realized that his fate was already decided, he suddenly changed his tone. "Ok well

52

go ahead you fuck. Why don't you just pull that there trigger and see where it lands you."

And then – Pop. The first blast almost caused me to drop the gun. The round caught him in the shoulder, though I was aiming for his head. He fell back in pain. He then faced up as I approached over him, this time closer so that I was sure it would finish the job. I just wanted this thing done. In defiance he spoke again.

"Yeah that's right! I did it. Fuck all of you! I don't apologize for anything. I done bodied so many niggas… It doesn't even matter anymore. I'm at peace, so be it. I'll never apologize for who I am. The only thing I'm sorry for is that I didn't take some of you out, before you got to me." He continued to writhe in pain. He then refocused his attention to me. "Or better yet, you – Ya fuckin' puppet sonofa…"

Pop. Pop. I didn't even allow him a chance to finish his speech. It was getting too ugly. What he had already admitted made him ugly in my eyes; too ugly to live. Here was a man who've been killing people himself for whatever reason. And now he expected mercy. The only sorrow I felt was that I didn't spare everyone's time and just pulled the trigger earlier. And then again, for reasons I still can't explain, I just emptied the remainder of the clip into his body.

When what I had just done finally hit me there was a silence that seemed to have lasted forever. Then hands clapping, followed by a few cheers interrupted the silence. And as vile as what had just taken place went down, I felt the most relieved afterwards. Light headed, but relieved. Then they all stepped out of the shadows. "Welcome aboard ya fuckin' murderer," one of the men humored.

"Yeah" I responded, shocked and feeling bewildered.

"Word up. You a straight block of ice G," another crewmember complimented.

"Yeah," I replied.

"Yo, enough of that," interrupted Grip. "They'll be plenty of time for introductions later. More matters to be done." Then he turned to T. "Yo T, take your cousin and show him the clean up."

"Gottdamn Grip! You wanna put him through the clean up too? His first night?!" protested T.

Grip didn't respond. He just turned to me. I paused as he searched my face. "Hey, cheer-up! It's done now. And you've proved yourself worthy. T told me you had it in you and he was right. You did hesitate at first, but who doesn't their first time?"

"Well I'm... Glad I could be of service," I replied, just beginning to recollect my senses. "This means I'm in?"

"Well for sure. You showed you had balls. And you're a relative of T, who's my best man. Nobody usually gets respect the first time with me no matter what. But T insisted we make you the exception. That's why I insisted you do what you did. Usually I let people just run with the crew before they do a job like that. You sure you didn't do this before?"

"Nah," I replied looking at the body.

"I'm only fucking with you man." Then he took notice of me staring at the once living remains. "Oh him? There's another condition with this guy you must go through before its official."

"What's that? Kill him again?" I humored.

He didn't laugh at all. "No. Clean up time. T will explain it to ya. And with that, I bid you peace out fellas." He and the others left, leaving T and myself behind for the unthinkable to me at the time.

"T, what do we have to do?"

"We've got to get rid of the body," he replied.

"Oh. Like put him in the trunk?"

"Well yeah. But first we're gonna have to play autopsy."

"What? Trevor. No! Please don't tell me what I think it is. I can't do that."

"There is no can't. You just do. Or we all might be fucked."

"Shit! Why?"

"Cause it's my night tonight. And you're with me as the guest of honor, so... No more questions man. Please." he seemed a bit frustrated. "This fucking Grip man. Sometimes, I wonder what he be thinking."

"I know where you're coming from. I only knew him for maybe only 10 minutes of my life and part of me was tempted to shoot him too."

T began to laugh as he pondered the joke. "I hear you cous. C'mon. Let's get to work. I want to catch the late programs on T.V."

***

After the whole night was finished, I knew I would never be quite the same. Not physically, emotionally, nor mentally. And my spirituality was definitely in question. I remember T handing me over a pair of rubber gloves, a dark rubber raincoat, and a saw. He showed me wear to cut the man and I nearly passed out a few times. From there we loaded the body parts in a bag and threw it in the trunk next to a few concrete blocks. We then drove to an undisclosed location in the park and cut off all the lights. Quickly we struggled with the few concrete blocks and placed them in the bag with the dead guy's remains. We stabbed a few holes in the bag so that the water would faster assist with the decomposition. We carried the bag to the edge of the park lake and then 1- 2 - 3 heaved the bag about 4 ½ feet into it. This was all done as quickly as possible.

We didn't say a word to each other in the car. Unbelievable was the only word that would come to mind. All I expected before I even came along on the trip was to get into the act of doing a few hustles with T. I end up coming out a murderer in cahoots with a group of killers. I remember starting to think of T in the light of – *this guy was a killer? T? Jeez.* It's still hard to believe, but then why not? Just look at me.

When we finally got home it was late in the middle of the night. I just walked in with my mind in a spin. I was mostly thinking about the repercussions that our act may bring, but T seemed the same.

"Damn!" said T as he turned on the T.V. "I missed my Program." He then threw the remote on the couch and headed upstairs. "Goodnight Cous."

"Goodnight T," I replied as I watched him go up the stairs. I couldn't sleep that night. So I tried to watch T.V. to get the events out of my mind. It helped only a little. From that night I was on edge. I was a nervous and paranoid wreck. I kept looking through the blinds to see who was outside. If the phone rang, or the mailman knocked on the door, I would think it might be the police. I even checked the news obsessively. Nothing. It's safe to say that my anxiety level was at a total chaos. I thought of God and if he was going to send me to hell. I thought of my mother and how much she would've disapproved. And as I began to look at T in sort of a different shade now, I thought that him and the others might kill me or rat me out; or both. Even the thought of getting back at that asshole boss Mr. Killough, which I really wanted to do, had long left my mind until T brought it up again sometime after.

"Yo broham," T called out from the kitchen one day, fixing himself a left over turkey sandwich.

"Sup," I answered?

"Whatever happened to that racist muthaphucka you wanted to do?"

"Uh – who?"

"You know who clown! The one who got you laid off that job on that bullshit."

"Oh. I dunno."

"Nah?" He came out of the kitchen now with a plate of food and a cola. "Well that's a shame kid."

"Hmph."

That was the only response I had at the moment. Here I was just trying to get over the last ordeal. And here he is suggesting another one. I was just trying to blow if off, but he just kept going.

"Yep. I mean that's a shame you would let him get away with that."

"Oh. Nah, well… It's alright. History anyway."

"History huh? Yeah I hear you. You're gonna let that nigga just punk you huh?"

"Hold on T." I turned to face him. "Where is this coming from? I mean, since when are you so interested all of a sudden? Before it was – fuck him. Now you want to push this thing?"

"I've always been concerned Non. You're my family. And I just hate to see good people get fucked over."

"Yeah well, I wouldn't exactly say I'm a good person at this point. I'm still trying to forget of a certain deed done recently?"

"Nonsense Non. You have a good heart. It was just the circumstance. You wanted in, so I brought you in. Finito. Don't dwell on it."

But I did dwell on it. I started to get frustrated. I didn't want any part of this. I was no murderer and especially not for hire. My thoughts were – h*ow dare Trevor trick me into this shit? What was he really doing to me?*

"Well I can't help but to dwell on it T," I replied with an obvious frustrated tone. "Every day I'm thinking there's going to be some serious repercussions from that shit. Ya know? I'm still pissed off that you'd trick me and then have the nerve to say forget about it."

"Tricked you?!"

"Yeah! Tricked! I mean, I'm thinking we're gonna sell guns or some shit. The next thing I realize is that I'm dumping a body!"

"Hey. Lower your voice."

"That was a fucked up thing to do T."

"Yo, Non…"

"I mean that was a real fucked up thing to…"

"ENOUGH," T yelled out. "First of all, lower your gottdamn voice! These houses have thin walls. Second, just stop bitching all together. You're the one who wanted in. Now you're in. I mean, okay, I'm sorry they went under those circumstances. I didn't mean for that. That was just Grip's thing. What can I say? He's an asshole. But I get you in and this is how you repay me? By accusing me of tricking you?"

"Alright T. I see where you're going. I get it. Just…"

"No. No I don't think you get it Non." He turned off the television, placed the remote next to his plate, removed the tray of food from off his lap and placed it on the coffee table. "This is why I asked about that hick boss in the first place. Just to see if you were alright with this. Yet, three fucking weeks passed and you're still on edge. Now, I don't know what issues you need resolved inside your mind about this, but you have to be aware of a few things."

"What's that?" I asked, still a bit frustrated, but also listening carefully.

"Well I'll tell you, you smug smartass muthaphucka."

"That's funny T."

"I'm serious man. Listen to me. You're in. Ok? That's it. I don't think you know what that really means. It means that for one, you've got to stop acting like you're fucking guilty of something. It can be read all over you. I don't want to hang out with you in front of my associates and you got this guilty aura around you, because all that'll compromise is your ability to work. If they smell guilt, they won't understand. You understand? They'll only take it the wrong way. Then they'll start to evaluate you."

"You mean like a test."

"Indeed Non. And I don't know if that was just a sarcastic remark, or if you finally understand, but I'd hate to think you still don't see the seriousness of this. Ok? If Grip has to give you a second look and even thinks you're not with us he's going to have you killed. And then, he might have me killed. You understand?"

"I wasn't being sarcastic T. I understand."

"Good." He picked up the tray again from the coffee table and placed it back on his lap. And then, with the remote in his hand he added, "Non. I know this is hard man. Again, I apologize for the severity of this shit. I realize you maybe gotta resolve some issues on the matter within yourself, or God, or whatever. Just remember, that what's done is done. Don't fuck around and bring on the unnecessary."

"Hey. You don't have to tell me T. I'm straight. I guess I was just trippin' because everything went so fast man. My head was spinning. I had no idea you were involved in such a thing man. It was just like, right before my eyes, you had turned into some cold-blooded monster."

"Well, I ain't a monster Non. I'm the same old T. But, I understand where you're coming from. You'll get over it Non. I promise. It'll become like nothing. Just stick around, observe and learn as you go. You'll be alright."

"Hm."

"Oh, by the way," he reached into his robe pocket, pulled out a white envelope, and then tossed it to me. "Now that we've got through that speech; Here's your first pay."

Inside were more 'Benjamin Franklin' bills than I'd ever held in my hands. It was actually $4,000. As I pulled the money out, I was almost hypnotized. I didn't know bills could seem to glow such an emerald green when held in a different light.

"Oh shit! T!" I exclaimed in marvel. That's all that could come to mind at that point.

"Yep. Your bonus is included in that too. The whole crew gets the same reward."

"T, this is unreal."

"Believe it fammo. That's just the beginning. I've got more to show you, but later. Just enjoy the cash and don't spend it all. Compliments of the Org. We're high priced enforcers. We're mixed up in a couple things Non. I'll tell you about it later. It's just in our tradition to bless the newcomer. Stay tuned bro. In due time."

He then turned back on the TV and began to search through the channels. I didn't know what to say. I did know that at that point, my anxiety was cured. Just like that. And in time, he did explain the basics of the thing.

I soon learned that we were the top hitters for this group of high-powered, yet low key and murderous organization. This organization was known as none other than 'The Org'. I learned that we were just one of many other crews. Matter of fact, we operated a bar with one of them. However, they dealt with mainly the moneymaking aspect. Extortion of other less powerful crews and businesses, whom were not associated with the org and whom operated on Org turfs, while working the books was the stuff they dealt with mainly. Yet, although we worked with each other, we were like night and day. Usually they operated during the day and we at night. All that we were were the 'code red' guys. The last resort. The guys who came in after the warnings. I hated it at times, cause' some of it got messy.

Now, Grip was the leader of our crew because he had earned his stripes. He was the only one in our crew who was an actual direct Org member. We were just the

guys on his payroll, but still had the benefits. Sort of like a temp job. Really just murder-for-hire guys when it came down to it. If you were a crew just running around without an Org representative then you were just pulling minor jobs. So the significance of Grip in our group was that we held a lot of weight. And Grip really looked over the affairs of both crews. He'd go over the books and made sure everything was right. All and all only a few crews did what we did. We were supposed to be diehard, but I was a nervous wreck for a long time before I began to adjust. At the same time, I had to make certain that the others couldn't read that. I had to pretend I enjoyed it for fear of how they might react if they sensed otherwise. Eventually though, I did enjoy it. The money was well. Fuck the 9-5 grind. T and I even went so far as to kidnap my ex- Asshole boss Mr. Killough just for fuck's sake. I ended up losing my temper and played baseball with his head though. I just wanted to give him a 101 on lying on folks like me. It was too severe for him to survive it. Oh well.

Yeah, I definitely got more comfortable with the work as time went on. And there were times I didn't even have to be there, but I still got paid. I got used to the higher life. Soon, nothing that would scare or seemed too rash for the average Joe would scare me. The crew became my family and I their brother. Our whole outlook on life was that of a bitter man facing the electric chair. We were untouchable. We had our own credo on life and death that helped me to get through a lot of the trying tasks. It was framed in our homes. It read:

[Death is inevitable – but life is forgettable. So if that day one's forced out early from the others – it only meant that he got a head start my brothers]

A late member wrote it. I felt it was the most beautiful message in its simplest form.

Chapter IV – Get a 'Grip'

My first year in was mainly spent doing a lot of adjusting. I surprised myself as to how well I adapted in such a short period of time. There were only seven heavy jobs that year in which I only partook in four. So, that made the load easier on me. For the most part it was just help run the bar, collect money, lift weights, get with the ladies and hang with Trevor. That was it. From time to time Grip would show his face, throw his weight around and then leave. You would never see him around unless he was either counting money with the other Org members, or pulling a job himself. This was cool, cause' I wasn't the only one who didn't like his demeanor most times. He'd always eyeball you as if to intimidate. You know. Just like you would fucking do to a kid. I mean, he'd come through and just stare members of his own crew down, leading one to believe that he either had something in store for em', or that you did something you weren't supposed to do, or the all-time 'what da fuck you doing over here' glare. At first I thought it was just me, but then T told me that it was just the way he was. That it wasn't so much to scare folks as it was just a front for his character. In either case, I didn't know if this psychological mind game may have had worked on some of the other guys, but I did know that it had no affect on me whatsoever. It didn't bother me at all much, and I wouldn't be surprised if any one else was really anything but annoyed. In truth he was really an alright guy, whom just at no time wanted to chance the appearance that he was softening up. However, I wouldn't blame any who knew of this if they were just a bit intimidated, due to his stature, size and animal like aggression. For the most part he was a stand up fellow, and I'll never forget the day he saved my life.

It was New Years Eve 2001 and everyone was getting ready for the big party. Some bashment' the guys were throwing in the neighborhood. T and the others hadn't arrived yet. I was the only one left at the bar. I figured that from there I'd just head straight to the party. Then, around closing time, Grip came in.

"You still here Nigga?" said Grip, as he flicked the switch, turning on the lights that I had just before turned off.

"What up man? I was just closing down and what not." I replied.

"Shit. The bartender should be doing that," he reasoned back as he made his way to behind the bar in search of a drink.

"Yeah I know. Said he wanted to leave early to get to his home on time to prepare for the New Years, or some shit like that."

"Heh. Alright, I'll help you close." He took off his coat and threw it on the barstool. "But let's be quick about it. I got to meet my baby girl. You know. The one you tried to bag sometime ago?"

"You mean she's your girl now?"

"Very funny."

"I'm just buggin' man. You know I wasn't trying to push up on 'the man's' wife."

"I know. I know. I been knew you were T's cousin. I just wanted to fuck with you to see where your heart was at. But you remained cool. Even now." He took a moment to pause and then turned to pour another drink. "But it's a good thing you did though, cause' I'd of hate to bring it to you."

We both laughed. I had to laugh because it just tickled me how true that notion might've been.

There wasn't much to close, as I was almost finished before he first came in. So we just took a few drinks and bullshitted about the life. We talked about all sorts of things. Like how he was planning a baby boy soon, and how he might marry his woman. I just listened and expressed to him how lucky he was. For that first time I saw a more humanitarian side to Grip. Perhaps it was the alcohol, or perhaps it was the thought of starting a family. By the time he had finished sharing his philosophy on how life should be he seemed like a whole different person. It was almost hard to believe that this guy was part of something sinister.

Then I got a page from T telling me that they were no longer coming to meet at the bar, because they were already at the party setting up. "Fuck it. We were leaving anyway," stated Grip, as we locked up.

As we headed out towards his car, Grip all of a sudden just stopped. "What? Forget your keys?" I asked in humor.

"Nah – I..." he paused, seemingly staring in one direction. "You got your gun?"

As he asked of my gun, I began to sense something was wrong. "Nah, it's – it's in the bar." I started to grow a bit alarmed. "Wh – why?"

"In the bar?" There was a confused look on his face. "What kind of a bonehead..?" He paused and caught himself. He then calmly mumbled out the side of his mouth, like a ventriloquist. "Look, but don't look too hard."

"Ok." I acknowledged in uncertainty, looking through the corner of my eyes.

It was a car just parked about a block off with its headlights on. Nothing seemingly unusual since it was dark out, except that the high beams were on. Pretty soon we couldn't help but to stare at it like two mesmerized deer.

Then Grip continued. "I feel that's the same car that some dudes were 'ice-grilling' me from before I walked in the bar.

"Word?" There was a pause. The glare from the automobiles' headlight made it hard to make out its full description. "Let me go get my gat."

"Do that," he motioned, still staring into the light.

As I turned to nonchalantly head back to the bar, the headlights go out and the car starts to cruise down the block towards us. I turned to witness two masked men hanging out the window with pistols drawn as the car swerved closer to the curb. Grip ducked, drew his gun and yelled for me to go. The slight alarm I was feeling now began to manifest into an overwhelming panic.

I ran down the block ducking as the car screeched after me firing shots; Very loud shots. My heart felt as though it wanted to explode out of my chest. I couldn't believe that I was being shot at. I panicked in truth. As the car pulled up next to me I ducked and tried to use the parked cars separating me from my assailants as a shield, while almost simultaneously ducking and running back in the other direction, trying to get back to where Grip was. Next thing I know, I heard the car doors open, and then felt a bullet graze my calf. I stumbled on my knees trying to crawl to hide between more parked cars. And then, as I tried to limp away, I heard the footsteps coming. It soon felt as though they were right up on me. I wanted to just stop crawling and give up, for I felt I was dead for sure. What were they waiting for though? Were these sadistic bastards trying to savor the moment? *Do it!* This I almost cried out from my mind, as there was a brief pause. Then, more shots were fired, but now they were trading them with Grip. I then crawled across the street thinking I was going to catch another bullet for sure. But, I didn't. When I got across the street from the melee, I picked up and limped down the block and around the corner. Now, I felt that I was out of harms reach. And the thought that I had eluded certain death also activated a sense of calm. I still felt scared, but I also felt a rush. The rush of surviving a deadly ambush.

So now I felt as though I was home clear. Only, the sense of calm that reclaimed me allowed me to come back to the realization that I could not have eluded death without the help of Grip. He saved my life, yet he himself was still in harms way. And here I was around the corner ready to jet out of there. But what could I do? I was unarmed and wounded. There was the great temptation to continue my exodus to safety. However, I didn't want to just leave him behind either. I felt that it just wouldn't be right. So, I took a peek back around the corner, I guess to see if he was fending well. I spotted him crouched behind a car firing away, as the two gunmen themselves were taking cover from car to car, yet still closing in.

Grip seemed to be holding his own for that moment. He was trading shots for shots with his pursuers. He was literally 'shooting the fair one' with both men. He didn't look scared, nor either jumpy. Instead, he looked determined. But then suddenly, as if was his destiny, he couldn't seem to fire anymore. He had ran out of ammunition and decided to make a run for it. He took off down and across the street towards my direction. I though that if he could've only swung that corner he'd have made it. Of course then I would have had to have been running. However, Grip doesn't even make it halfway. The two gunmen emerge from there cover and fire a few carefully placed shots, all of which hits Grip in the back. I watched him stagger and slow down until he could no longer move forward and fell on his knees. There he just waited. His eyes then caught mine peering from behind the block. He started to smile as though he was amused that I was still around, or as if seeing a long lost pal and speechless. Of course, that was most likely just the blood draining from his system. This alone was too much for me. And I felt murderously frustrated that I could do nothing more, but watch.

I heard them approaching and so must've he, yet he didn't attempt to move, or flinch, or even turn to see his makers. He just closed his eyes as they approached. Again, I just wanted to run out there and do something; but what? One of them then presses the nozzle directly on top his head. The other taunting him and asking if any last words. All this time Grip is still staring in my direction. He opens his mouth to say something; possibly something smart, but never gets a chance. The gunman just pulls the trigger and blows his head apart. Then the other gunman laughs and shoots what's left of his head. Then they both just kept shooting him in the face. After that, they just laughed and dropped a gold chain on him, taking off towards their getaway car. I staggered over to his body after the assailants raced away and almost heaved when I saw what was left of Grips face. It still haunts me. I wanted to cry admittedly. But as I heard sirens, I picked up the gold chain the two killers left and staggered off.

As I headed home I naturally just kept flipping the whole gruesome scene in my head over and over again. What if I had had my gun? Would Grip still be alive? Would I be dead in place of Grip? Would we just both be dead? What were Grip's last words going to be? Was he going to say something smart, or was he actually going to rat to the killers that I was still around? The whole thing just played out in slow motion. Damn it all. I felt I had to get to T and the crew. They had to be the first to know, and then maybe they could help the burning sensation I felt from the bullet lodged somewhere in my calf.

As I headed for the nearest station I could here the sirens getting closer. The desire for a car began to grow as I limped onto the train. I had then rapped a bandanna, which I happened to have in my pocket, around the wound so to stop the bleeding, and to avoid attracting attention. Good thing it was late night, so there were hardly anyone on there. By the time I reached home I paged T with the 'code red' and waited. My leg started to feel more numb with each passing minute. I worried erratically at the thought of a possibility of having my leg amputated. The thought soon vanished when I saw T's car pull into the driveway from the living room window. I signaled by the door that all was alright. He then hurriedly exited his vehicle and stepped into the house. I do a double check for any type of law-lights before I lock back the door.

"Wsup?! What?!," T began, as he was well aware of what 'code red' meant.

"T," I respond as I try to ease back onto the chair to relieve my leg. "T, these guys rolled up on us man. They rolled up on us."

"Rolled on who?!"

"Me and Grip. They…"

"Shit you're hit?! Let me see."

He had only then just begun to realize I got wounded. I showed the wound as I continued. "Man. They killed Grip man. They killed him right in front of me."

"Damn man!" responded T. He was showing obvious hurt as he reached for a chair to sit down.

There was a brief moment of silence, and then I continued again. "It was an ambush man. These two Niggas just rolled up – and, and then they were just gunning for us. I thought I was going to die T. And – Grip, he saved my life man. He just – but, I couldn't save him though man. I couldn't save that Nigga T."

"Geez." That was momentarily the only response from Trevor. After about another 1minute pause. "Fuck! Yo, listen. We gotta see about that wound. It don't look serious, but I dunno."

"Yeah. Oh and –" I pulled the gold chain out and showed it to T. "They left this."

T quickly grabbed, and then examined the item. And then his face started to show rage. He then began to snort out obscenities. "It's that Fag Richie Rich!!" Then he snapped the chain and placed it in his pocket. "Yo. I can't begin to tell you how dead them Niggas are!"

"Who da fuck is Richie Rich?" I asked, also growing furious.

"This Nino type drug kingpin that the Org gave more than enough warning to. That stubborn 'Wankster' wants to play like he won't budge. He's FUCKED! He probably just somehow found out that our shit was Org affiliated and wanted to send a message."

"A message huh?"

"Yeah. That's why whomever those fucks he hired left the chain with their trademark on the medal."

"So we just go fuck em' up."

"For sure, but – this not no small time drug crew we dealing with."

"What're you saying?"

"I'm saying we're talking about a serious war. I'm saying we might have to close down the bar for a minute."

"So be it. We backed by the Org."

"Nah. We just they affiliates, in which case, the Org might probably ask why they should get involved since it didn't hit them home. I mean, true Grip was a representative, but it's all a matter of if they're willing to go risk a war with the Richie Rich's drug crew over one mishap. Ya know – on some bypass shit. All Richie has to say is he's been setup or some shit like that."

"You must be fucking kidding me!"

"I kid you not Non. They know that Richie knows not to fuck with them direct. Or so they feel, being a big power and all. This type of shit happens all the time. Take out aggression on the goons to send them a message, who'd care. How you think them stories of missing Niggas from other crews be coming true? Hell, Richie probably doesn't even know that an Org rep got hit."

"Well if he did he naturally wouldn't care. That's messed up T. I thought them stories were just jokes half the time. Myths. Families disappearing and shit? Kids and all? That Nigga Richie is not a drug lord. That

Nigga's a monster. And how I'm feeling right now with all this shit you're talking, I'm going to turn that monster of a being into a ghost."

"Hmm. Well we could still plead our case to the Org. Present the chain anyway and tell them of Grip. Who knows? They might send the word."

"And if they disapprove T?"

"That's the gamble Non. They disapprove and we can't touch him. And then fuck it, cause' Grip was their man anyway."

"T. Approval or no approval, this Richie character that you just told me about will become nothing more than a specter. I almost got killed. Them Niggas had me scared to death, running like a bitch and to top that off, rendered me helpless to watch a standup guy get killed virtually right in front of me. That could've been me – you, or any of us. And they got the one who saved my life – and laughed. Nobody lives T."

"I'm with you 'fam'. It was personal from when you sent the 'code red'."

"Indeed."

I was seething with such frustration and anger to the point that I forgot all about the burning wound. We took a ride to an in-house non-licensed doctor T knew. It was nothing more than a flesh wound. Soon after, I was back home and just pondering thoughts. This time it wasn't so much thoughts of revenge than a reflection on what I've actually become. To make it short, I thought of myself in the days before the crew as a pathetic pussy who wouldn't kill a man if he had stabbed me himself. Back then I had too much thoughts of rationality and repercussions. But now, somehow over my time spent with the crew, I realized that I could kill in good conscious. It wasn't hard really. Maybe I always could've. I guess all I needed was the right opportunity. Most of the guys were underworld gangsters, thugs, defiant merchants, etc. In a twisted way it helped me to cope with my own possible fate. I figured that since I was a part of a killing crew – then I was no better. Just part of the food chain that'd eventually get ate up by either others such as myself, or the law. Whichever came first was just a matter of time. In my reality, this whole thing began to feel like almost nothing. Almost. And then, as soon as I thought of my mother, more innocent times long past came to mind. I felt my more inner soul from ago trying to rationalize things. Then more thoughts came to me. Who was I? I could never see me doing this before. How do I know whom I've hurt or affected, whether somebody's parents, or somebody's child? Did I voluntarily damn my own soul? And when I decide to get tired of this – can I claim it back? Here I am ready to go kill this Richie myself if I have to. I would've never had the balls before. Sinisterly I felt pride in being what I was. I knew I was dangerous. I even began to feel more so than some of the other's in the crew and they knew it. They knew I'd go where some might draw the line. I would defy anything – the Law or the Org. I only drew the line at love and children. I would sacrifice neither. Yet that night, when I thought of the old times and my mom, I could only weep. The rest of that night, as I lay in bed, I out the lamp and I wept in darkness.

***

So the word was sent and a war broke out. It was horrible – for our enemies that is. We just kept striking fierce. The Org stepped back and allowed only a few of its affiliates to send Richie a message. People were dropping left and right. A few good times I saw my opportunity to strike upon Richie, but to do so would have been instant suicide. So I laid low. We went back and forth with this crew whom I underestimated. It wasn't that they were more ruthless. It was that they were just that large. This feud we had went on for months with the

71

bombings, the kidnappings, the street slaughters and raids.
It was an uneasy sort of event in that no one knew when
and if they were being targeted. Our advantage was that
we were so on the low, we could hardly be found. Only
those that were known were targets. Richie's crew was
well known. Just go to where ever they were known to be.
Soon the war got old, and when the Org decided to fully
step in the war had ended almost overnight. It wasn't long
before Richie had to go into hiding. His own crew
eventually turned on him. Some, becoming affiliates
themselves. There were rumors that some of his top guns
had exposed his hideout in exchange for leniency. It was
at that moment I realized how big the Org was. Who were
they? They obviously weren't just some mob type outfit.
They were like this gigantic ghost of a secret society
whose might seemed to rival government agencies. An
underground enterprise with even some righteous virtues
of a modern day Robin Hood.

Upon speaking to T and a few others I started to
get a more clearer picture of the Org. One learned that
they funded only urban community projects. These
projects that they funded were also marked. This meant
that it was a safe haven. There was absolutely no selling
of drugs or any narcotics on Org turf, which of course also
meant no drug gangs. No pimps. No prostitution. No
anything that was considered negative vibes towards
whatever tenants paying there. They basically made the
areas safe. I mean it was still urban. There were still kids
that could hang around, play loud music and shoot dice
and what not. Even smoke weed. As long as there were
no shootouts for other than defending yourself or block.
Any crew into narcotics had to do so away from the safe
havens and still needed to kick back a percentage to the
Org. That's it. You couldn't have beef with someone and
start shooting at a park full of kids. They were like safe
projects and the Org silently watched everything. If they
felt something was a threat to whatever they considered an

investment then they stepped in and gave warning. They seldom had to do this though. Of course you had knuckleheads every now and then who would disregard the Org and break its' laws, but then they obviously had a death wish and preferred it so. So this is where their wide network of affiliates came in.

The Org used its' affiliates to make sure things were right. You would think it was the young guys over at the corner ice-grillin that you'd have to be wary of when in fact; it could be the senior citizen types playing chess in the park. You just didn't know. A dangerously calm environment within a community. So then what of those govt. agencies that looked into unlawfully operated organizations and groups? I'd imagine they could only bust affiliates. Bust the muscles. Hell, the Org might've been a secret government ran agency themselves designed to restore the peace beyond boundary of laws. Who knew? How else could one explain their rumored ties into corporations, jurisdiction influences and the likes? Yet and still – all rumors. They might've just been another super powerful crime family that the feds would disband at any moment. A seemingly do-good organization compromised of mostly us minorities.

So eventually, the only thing my crew had to do was go and bring the crack kingpin to justice. His whereabouts now exposed, his minions depleted. Yes, I felt very excited about going in and getting him ourselves. Not for the joy of killing or anything like that. Just payback. Payback for a fallen leader and the bullet that touched my leg.

We rolled up between some cut blocks in Brownsville. Just me and an associate I'll refer to as Pipe. We called him pipe, cause' his side occupation was Plumber. A quiet and reliable guy. The word was that he was hiding out in one of the housing complex apts. Just when I thought to myself we'd be parked here all day, out he comes out of this building with two bodyguard types and steps into his Benz.

"Bingo." Pipe mumbled.

We pulled off and didn't come back till' later that night. Didn't see the Benz, so we waited in the car. "Hey Pipe," I started.

"Sup?"

"How we gonna do this?"

"Chu' mean?" he replied as if not wanted to be bothered with talk. Like I said, he was a quiet guy, but not the type you didn't trust. He was quiet, yet cool. He hung out with the crew and usually responded with abbreviated words that weren't meant to be abbreviated. "We're gonna kill him. Him and whoever's in the way."

"Well, I know that, but – how are we going to go about doing this?"

"Well, let's see. When we see him roll up, one of us go'ver there and gunnem' down."

"One of us?"

"Yeah." He turned to face me now. "Someone's got to getaway drive."

"True."

"And since you're the rookie, and I'm already at the wheel..." He produced to me a 9mm semiautomatic pistol as he grinned slightly. "Here you go kiddo."

"Oh word?" I said, sounding uneasy. I was still a little jumpy when it came to these things, but I had to keep my cool.

Then around 1am the Benz rolls up. I roll the mask down over my face and rack the pistol. I'm expecting him to be accompanied by the same two goons, but instead he comes out with this real fine lady. We watched as they laughed and played around with each other as they made their way for the stoop.

"Now," said Pipe, sharply.

I ducked out the passenger side door and crouched behind it, inching myself closer from behind car to car, until I felt I was close enough. Then, when I popped up in front of him, he looked shocked at first, but he knew. We glared at each other for about two long seconds; me at his amazed expression, him at my eyes through the mask.

"Delivery from the Org," I stated, as I leveled the barrel and parted pigeons. The lady friend he was with started to scream. "Shut up bitch!" I growled, but she wouldn't stop. I paused wondering if to kill her.

"Do her!" Pipe's voice echoed from out of the car and down the block.

I leveled my piece again, slowly aiming it at her head. I remember thinking – 'I don't want to do this'. But then, suddenly, she stopped and only whimpered. "Please, Please" she cried. "I just met him today."

I slowly lowered my gun as sirens could be heard far off in the background. "Fuck! Let's get out of here," yelled Pipe. I took off into the car and we rolled out.

Soon as we felt we escaped the crime scene and the threat of police, Pipe spoke out again. "Da Fuck is wrong with you?"

"What? The girl?"

"You can't be soft man. You can't be soft. She could identify the car, your size... All that shit. She could mean 25-Life for you and you aint' do her!" He sucks his teeth in disgust. "Man, please. That's not cool Nigga. That shit's not cool at all. Fuck it. I'm not taking no chances. We've got to ditch this car now."

"Now muthaphucca?!"

I've never seen Pipe so intense. He must've really been upset. We hopped out the vehicle and took everything that could link us. We wore gloves before we entered car so there were no fingerprints. We took the guns, disassembled each part and scattered them about in the drains and garbage. Made sure we took all our personals, like a wallet or ID. Only thing incriminating was our clothes. We took off our shirts and ski mask and set in on fire in a garbage can.

The shoes and pants we left on. So now we're moving quickly down the block looking for the nearest train station in our tank tops. After that, Pipe seemed to relax a bit. Good thing we used a stolen car.

"Non," he continued, "I do not know if I can fuck with you on this type of thing again."

"Don't say that Pipe. It's a learning experience." I responded, uneasy and tired.

He then laughed. "Da fuck was all of that dodging and weaving tween' cars and shit? What're you a fuckin' action figure? I could barely contain myself in the ride."

"Being cautious," I humored back, a bit more relieved. We rode back the rest of the trip in silence.

So that was that. Later things were just back to normal. And soon I was known as a top hitter in my squad. They said I had become more ferocious than before. More bold; crazy even. And I was. I earned my stripes, but a long time passed before anything happened again.

Chapter V – What does a road trip & a Mob hit have in common?

"You got the appropriate info?" asked T.

"Yeah," I replied.

"Enough money?"

"Yeah T."

"The contact? Cause' you know you gotta be sure..."

"Yeah Nigga!" I replied, getting a little testy. "I got it."

"Alright, alright. Just if any problems give the call."

"You got it T."

I was on my way a few hours across the highway to exchange firearms for cash to our contact. He moved some hours away south into Pennsylvania, which was of no convenience to us, but nonetheless he was our man. We had other contacts, but T stressed the fact that he was still 'our guy', and that it's just good business. He also suggested that a nice drive through the scenic routes were relaxing. I, myself was fond of long drives, so I couldn't really complain.

So I'm off down the road a few hours into the night with a jeep suburban full of heavy expensive artillery. It was a very big order done once or twice a year. Lockup if I'm pulled over for sure. This was the only thing that made me uneasy, so you can imagine that I nearly caught a heart attack when I saw flashing sirens behind me. But when I pulled out of the way they flew right passed me. 'Be easy' – I told myself a few times, coupled with the fact that I was growing hungry. The nearest diner was said to be just off some exit onto a dismal route. Just great. But, I did find it.

As I pulled into the parking lot, one couldn't help but to notice that the diners looked like a cowboy coral front. I paused for a minute watching through the windshield as these hillbilly, Klansman looking folk entered into the diner. It seemed pretty packed too. Was it cause' it was a Friday night? I didn't see not one black folk. Hell, not even an Indian. Part of me wanted to pass for the nearest McDonalds, but then I thought 'why should I?' I'm hungry. Aint shit worry me. Almost disgusted with myself for debating it in the first place. I came out of the car and headed into the diner. Looked up at the sign it read: 'The O.K. Grill.'

"Ok," I said to myself as I entered.

Now music was playing, Country of course. And it was a little noisy from the crowd. Folks shooting pool off the corner; Band on the stage; People at the tables and at the bar. But I paused at the door for a brief moment, when for the longest second, most eyes were on me. As I walked in, most seemed to have turned away, but I could still feel the eyes. 'Fuck this,' I thought to myself. I ignored and continued on.

By the time I sat at the order bar, everyone seemed to have gone back to what they were doing, with the exception of a few glares here and there. I just glared back and even winked at the ones who seemed interested in a stare down contest. Heck, some of them were drunk and probably aint' hang my kind in years. At least that's what I reasoned. Besides, I've got all my confidence in my pistol, tucked away in the small of my back, in detectible to the ignorant eye.

"Sir," I called out to the barkeep, who I noticed knew I was there signaling for him, yet paid me no mind. When he finally did come over he just looked at me and put one arm on his hip with a look on his face that made it seem I was pestering him.

"What?" he snapped.

"What?! Chu' mean what? I want something to eat! How long you've been working here?!" He paused there, still just staring. "Look blue eyes," I continued, trying hard not to fully break. "The faster you get that burger for me – the faster I'll leave."

Then he leaned over with that continued frost-eyed grill and mocked back, "Ok, Black eyes. How do you want it?"

I chuckled a bit. 'That's cute' – I thought to myself, still trying to hold back frustration. "Well damn done," I replied, as if adding more humor. I really wanted to level him.

He turned, took orders from the others and made small talk, then finally threw the burger on the grill. It was a good thing the grill wasn't in the back where I couldn't see what he was doing. I kept my eye on him and the preparation of my burger.

Soon after, I'm trying to finish my burger and stout in peace, while trying to take in the country band when these guys sitting next to me started talking reckless.

"Ya know," began one of the men to the other. "It's amazing how some outer towners think they can just waltz in here and think they're some kind of king".

Now this I hear. No one else could really hear what's said through the noise and music unless they were by me, but I knew whom the reference. Then, it was confirmed by me that they were when one of the other replied.

"Yeah, especially if he's some hood nigger off the streets. Thinks he can come in here and play bold."

By this time I was looking at them and they were looking at me.

"You referring to me?" I asked.

There was a brief pause and then one of them replied. "So what if we were? Coon."

Then I retaliated. "You feel safe in here huh you fuck. How bout' we step outside so I can slit both of your fucking throats huh? Billy Badass." I took another sip of the brew and there's a pause. "Fuck this place," I declared, as I stepped outside the door. I then waited outside for 5 minutes in front my jeep finishing my drink. "Fucking punks," I cheered to myself, as I got in my jeep and pulled off. If I only got to kill people like that more often my job would be much easier. So you could imagine my startledness, followed by delight, at what happened next.

I'm continuing down the road and about a mile and a half from the bar, when a pickup truck rams me from behind. Twice.

"The fuck?!" was the response of my startled reaction.

Then the truck raced up next to the driver's side of my vehicle, forced me onto the dirt lane, and then pulled up in front of me. Out came Billy and two other guys. They were the guy whom he was with at the bar, who closely resembled Gomer pile, and some other fat smuck.

I stepped out of my vehicle with my pistol still concealed under my shirt and begun to ask. "What's this about?"

"It's about you comedian. You left before we could even think to tie you to a tree and give you a good old fashioned whippin'," he chuckled with the others.

I noticed that only Billy and Gomer had smirks on their faces thus far, but the other big guy they brought along never cracked a smile. He just stood in his spot. He must have something, cause he seemed too silently anxious.

"What?" I asked impatiently. I grew tired of waiting. "So what? You want to settle it here? The three of you?"

"Don't worry Nigger," answered Gomer. He had still a smirk. "All we want to do is tie you to the back of that there pickup, and drag your blackass down south." He then produced a rope. And with that, even the third fellow, Fatso, began to crack a nasty smirk as well.

"Ya – y'all serious?" I started to act as though I was panicky, just to make them think I had nothing to defend myself with. I also wanted to see how far I would play it out to find out if they were really intent on the supposed threat. "C'mon guys. All I wanted was something to eat. Y'all started it." I started to back up and look around as if looking for a place to run or yell help.

"Yeah, we started it boy," replied Billy. He had all the mouth. "And now we gon' finish it." His expression grew serious and then they all stopped smirking.

Fatso suddenly produces a revolver from out of his coat, but he didn't point it at me yet, guess figuring I was your average victim with no where to go. I figured now that they intended to try to do what they said.

At this, I faked as if I was going to run back for the jeep, and in the instance they took their first running step towards me I swung around with my defense mechanism and fired enough shots into the chest of the revolver holding fatso, thus exposing his cold heart to a more warmer feeling; Hot lead. The other two just froze in shock as I made my way towards them, and simultaneously fired one point blank into the head of the next victim, Gomer. He fell just a few feet from Billy. He wasn't important. It was the antagonizer, Billy, I was most interested in.

"Now Billy," I begun. "You didn't think I was just going to let you guys hang me did you?" I let out a serious smile.

"Da-Damn you. Don't kill me. Please," pleaded Billy, his face looking more concerned. "Please. We were only trying to scare you!" He now yelled in panic.

I only looked at him. "Billy. Billy calm down."

"I got children at home."

"Billy. Shhh," I attempted to hush him, while looking around for any potential witnesses.

"C'mon mister."

"Oh, now I'm mister. Billy, listen to me. Calm down and lower your voice, or I'm going to kill you."

"Whatever you want mister. Just don't kill me," he sniveled.

"Billy, get on your knees."

"Wha – why?"

"GOTTDAMMIT Billy!" my voice momentarily escalated in anger. "I'm gonna search ya and I don't want no problems. So do it!" As he quickly dropped on his knees I approached behind him. "Put your hands in the air," I ordered. Of course, he complied. He was beginning to shake from terror and I could see that clearly. I almost felt bad, but I also felt that if I didn't kill him, then it would have been a great injustice. Who knew how many times they've done this? I was protecting society. Besides, he was a witness, and we didn't leave witnesses around much.

"Now Billy…" I aimed the gun at the back of his head, not to his knowledge.

"Whatever you want mister," he sniveled.

"I'm going to leave you with these words, and then I'm going to leave you – in peace."

"Oh thanks mister." It's amazing how compliant one is when his life is in your hands.

"Billy, it's important that your kids don't grow up with the animosity that you have displayed to me this night."

"I agree sir."

"And it's important that they learn the value of respect for the next man, unless the next man doesn't show them any."

"I agree mister. Wholeheartedly. You have my word. I'll teach em' that."

I knew he was just babbling out of fear.

"What? Who said you was going to get the chance to tell them?" I asked coldly.

"Wha...?"

"I've got to kill ya Billy. How else would they learn what I've just said?" I chuckled.

"Aw mister," he turned to see the barrel aimed at his dome. "Wait mister!! Wai..."

"Pop-Pop." Point blank in the dome. He hits the ground and I pulled off.

"All this drama just to sell this shit?" I said to myself. I know... I know... I'm a sick man. I felt all right though, for I was able to cure three would-be violent men of their unrighteous views and tactics.

***

So I go back home. At this time I have my own place out in Bedford Stuyvesant, Brooklyn; not far from where I grew up. T and I are still tight, but it seemed we were tighter when we were under the same roof. It used to be all fun when I was there, even after I adapted to this whole Org thing. Then after Grip died, everything got more serious. The crew's attitude just didn't seem the same after a while. I mean, usually Grip did all the talking and had the place liven up. But now, we just sat there, each in own worlds just doing the upkeep duties of the night joint. Even T was beginning to seem more distant from even me at times; Like he had a lot on the mind. If every now and then I'd ask him was everything ok – he'd just say yeah and that no situation could get him down, long as the situation knew he was the boss. His humor.

I'm back home again. In the inner-city urban section and it's steadily improving. My place is quite cozy. It was your typical overpriced one bedroom apt. Got my bed, fridge, couch, T.V., radio and car. That's it. Nothing fancy. A lot of my stuff is still in boxes waiting to be packed away after months. My place always looked deserted, or like someone was just about to move out. But it doesn't bother me. I'm comfortable. I got the basic 'concrete jungle' necessities. All I could need. And I was saving my bread in case of any harsh weathers. Well almost all. Yep, nearing 27 years on this planet and I felt that I was doing exceptionally well for my age.

Women? Well there were always women. Women around the crew at parties; Women around the bar scene; Women; Women around the club our comrades ran. All gravy. Yet, I didn't have one of my own. You know? One I could care about. A wifey. This always appealed to me. I mean, there were ladies who were very appealing, and some who seemed genuine. The type you could take home to the family. But I never wanted to get too close to any of them. I was aware of my charm and I didn't want to charm some beautiful woman into my lifestyle. That was the one thing about this life. I feared it coming back to harm someone I loved, or truly cared about. That was something I think, I feared more than my own death.

So yes, I tried keeping my distance from the wifey-family idea. Hell, I was making my bread and having a few flings. And maybe, that's all I should've been happy with. It goes – you can't have everything. So then why when I saw this woman for the second time I couldn't stop thinking about her? It was the same woman I had that altercation over when I first saw Grip. Yep, it was Grip's lady. We met eyes again when I took a stroll through the mall. Like happenstance. She had on a pair of jeans and a jacket. She was in the homecare section apparently trying out a new bed. I watched her. She didn't see me. She looked like an image from above. The way the sunlight reflected through the window on her pretty face.

"Hey, how you doing?" I approached with a smile.

"Oh hi," she replied. She looked uncertain of me at first, but then an expression of familiarity. "You're Trevor's friend right?

Her smile grew warmer. I was only too thrilled that she remembered me. I felt like I was in high school again.

"Yeah. His cousin," I replied, not being able to help but to stare at her. "So how's life been for you?"

"It's been alright. Just trying to maintain," she answered, with that even warmer smile. "How have you been?"

"Never better." There was a pause and then I had to fill in quick. "Say, you doing anything after this?" I asked.

"Nah. Just browsing this house ware to see what fits."

"Oh that's cool. I just was wondering if you'd like to hang out sometime. Ya know – catch a movie or something." I knew I must've sounded lame, but through reading here face it didn't seem to matter.

"Sure," she replied. Again with that warm feeling I couldn't describe.

"Great. So – hmm – here's my number," I said, as I took out a pen and paper and jotted it down for her. "Make sure you call." I tried to crack a warm smile.

"Ok."

"Ok," I said. Then, catching myself stalling. "Hey, I'm gonna run now. Catch you later huh?"

"Later," she smiled, as I turned about and left. I thought it was love at first sight at the time, but she never called. And that left me a little frustrated. I ended up telling myself – "Fuck it. She's got her reasons. I'll see her again and then, who knows?" Should I have felt bad, lusting for 'the late' Grip's lady? Eh. I was over it.

The life continued, and I've made somewhat of a living out of my niche. The bar is being run and the money is average. Time rolls by and before you know it's only 2 ½ months before the New Years. At this point, everything is the same, but then what's the problem? I'm a little tired of it. I mean, on one hand this should've been the life. I got tight with the crew, money is alright, I'm living above average and at certain functions, the crew gets its props. But then, there's the gritty side. The messy side. It doesn't work out to be a man with a conscience in this business. The killings. Sure they were mostly on other guys who knew there was a price to pay for their actions, but I still had to cope with my demons somehow. It was just then that T came through the back door with a task handed from above.

"Yo. They want us to do a Record Exec." He started.

"Oh yeah?" I responded solemnly, not even looking up as I took a sip of whiskey. "What's the deal?"

"You won't even guess. The CEO of Locsmiff Records himself."

"You mean – Mr. Martini?!"

"No, Mr. Rodgers. Of course Mr. Martini."

"Hrmph." I paused a moment. I've never done a celebrity. This was kind of much. "T, how are we supposed to get to this man?"

"Group effort. The Org knows how this man moves somehow. They'll tell us where to be and when. Just hold tight."

"Okay," I responded, as I played with my drink. I thought for a moment, and then had to let T know how I felt. "Yo T."

"Sup?"

"How you feel about all this man?"

"What? The hit?"

"Yeah. Nah. I mean everything."

"I feel good. I mean I don't feel like doing this particular hit, among after others I didn't want to do, but eh." He shrugged his shoulders and then signaled for the bar help for a drink. "What ya gonna do? It's our lives." He downed half his liquor in one swallow. Then, he turned back to me. "Why do you ask buoy?"

"Ha." I let out an uneasy laugh. "It's just – don't you even feel your conscious fucking with you sometimes?"

"Nah. Nope. Never. I was made for this and this was made for me. I mean look at what we do. Yeah, you've got scores of folks who does this, but the majority of the world can't. I mean, check it." He leaned closer to me, looking obviously just a little affected by his drink. He proceeds by counting on his fingers each scenario. "You've got your everyday citizen, be it rich or poor just living out their oblivious lives. Right? Then you've got the wanna-be hustlers, not making no real moves, yet at the same time wants no parts of Babylon's working class society. Right? They even might bust their gun and do time for nothing. Then – then you have the real hustlers. The hardcore ones. Yeah, they're doing their thing, but who – who's badder than us?"

He was beginning to stutter a bit. A known Trevor trademark whenever he had too much to drink. Still, I was interested in what he had to say. He was more revealing this way, and it was a sight to see him philosophize on shit he usually wouldn't bother under sober conditions. He continued. "Then. You've got hitters. They bad right? They got all our qualities right? But – and get this – who backed by the Org yo? Ha ha." He lifted his glass in toast.

"Trevor. You're drunk man," I said as I eased back.

T was one of the coolest and most laid back guy I knew, but whenever he got drunk he looses it. After a few more, he only spitted out drunken rhetoric. So all though it was a bit humorous to see him in the state at times, I couldn't really talk to him that night.

"To us and the Org!" exclaimed T, as he lifted his glass in cheer.

"To the Org," I replied, as I returned the toast. Then, I just sat and watched the bar show as T left off to toast with the others.

Later on that night, while relaxing at home I pondered on the fact on how I didn't want to do this anymore. My conscience was really beginning to do a number on me. I stared at a picture of 'Black Jesus' on the wall and asked if I was going to hell. The eyes of the picture staring back at me almost seemed to nod yes back. "NO!" I strongly opposed to myself. I didn't want my flesh to devour my soul. What was I doing? I needed a break. I did not want to do this next God-awful task of doing in this CEO fellow and not even know the reason why. So the next day I shared my thoughts with T.

"What?!" asked T, in frustration mixed with disbelief. "Yo. What you talking?"

"I'm talking peace of mind T," I replied. "C'mon man. My nerves are shattered.
I feel shaky."

"Oh you do huh? Yo man, you're afraid? Now?
After all the jobs we pulled you
choose now to have a fucking conscience?"

"I know what it seems like T, but c'mon man.
I'm just asking that I sit this one
out. Just this one man." I watched for his expression. He didn't seem too happy about it. I knew that much. There was a long pause, and then I continued with the only reasoning there seemed left. "Please man."

T didn't say anything for a while after that. Just stood silent. Finally he responded. "Ok man. You know I don't really give a fuck. But I'm worried about you man. In that, if the Org were to ever know that you felt this way they'd literally leave you in a peace of mind. You know?"

"Huh, I know," I had to sigh in helpless frustration."

"Let's just keep this in house T'ween' me and you, alright Non? If anything, me and the boys will handle it."

"Aye. You don't have to tell me twice. Thanks T."

"Good. Don't mention it."

I sat down and started to watch the 'Nature' channel that T, of course, had on. There was silence as usual whenever this program came on. Then I had to ask.

"T."

"Sup?"

"You ever felt this way at any point in this career?"

"Nope."

"No? Not – not a little?"

"Nah. Seriously. No." he answered still fixed on the T.V.

"Oh. Ok."

I knew he might've been frustrated with the questions and just wanted to watch the T.V., but I also knew he usually told me the truth. And I mean, here we are in the same profession, but he scared me. How could a man not be affected by this? Nah. I thought to myself that he must have been lying. I turned and continued to watch the T.V. The program showed the lion chase down an antelope and eat it. Gruesome, yet all too familiar. My cousin Trevor, on the other hand, enjoyed those scenes more. Maybe cause' his actions closely resembled that of the lion's. No remorse at all, just the natural order and desire to kill and eat to survive.

***

This next assignment we had was to hit these two mob figures. It seems that they couldn't get along with their 'family'. One of them owned a car dealership in Queens and decided that he'd rather start looking out for his own interests. The other was his lackey. Guess one would ask, 'why punish the lackey?' The answer would be that he was secretly cooperating with the Federal Bureau of Investigations. Typical story of a guy, who tried to do extra shit, got busted and is now trying to save his ass. In my opinion, he can't even be blamed. Hell, if I knew I was facing over 30 years in fed time I'd drop a dime on the Org in a second. Call me what you will. The setup was perfect though. It was like two for the price of one. Both of them worked in the same vicinity and neither were the wiser of what was being plotted. So why would the mob hire outsiders on their family? Simple. To make it smell as something other than themselves. This is done often.

The job was given to me and whomever I wanted as a partner. Of course I chose T and of course he was cool with it. We decided that we'd do the owner first if we couldn't get both of them at the same time. It was just a matter of studying their movements and planning accordingly, which we felt shouldn't be hard to do, as it was a car dealership. All there was to it was to act as though intentions were towards purchasing a vehicle. So, work time.

I walked through the dealership door and was greeted by a sales associate. "Welcome sir. How can I help you today?"

"Uh yes sir, I'd like to purchase an automobile." I kindly answered.

"Sure thing. Good thing you've caught us right before closing. What did you have in mind, a new or used car?"

"Used, but not too used. Nah mean?" I humored.

"Heh heh. Sure thing buddy. Just come with me this way to our used car section and I'll get somebody to take care of you from that department. Ok?"

"Sure thing, uh… Vince," I squinted, so as to pronounce the words off his nametag as a sign of good character.

When we got to the used car lot I could see endless cars. The lot was huge and the fabulous array of different cars almost made me forget my true purpose for being there.

"Ok buddy. Just glance around and see what you like, and then somebody should be with you shortly," said Vince, as he made his way back to his dept. whilst taking a call on his cell phone.

"Thanks Vince."

I browsed around the lot from car to car trying to plot out what my next move should be. I've been to car dealerships before, but not to plot the execution of a murder. I'm now there browsing cars and thinking that my cousin and I should have planned this thing more better, while waving off sales reps, pretending that I needed more time. Perhaps it was a sign of us becoming sloppy.

Then finally, I decided that I'd just go on instinct. This had to be one of the most sloppiest of assignments that I'd ever performed.

"Hey uh..." I began, trying to read this other sales rep's nametag.

"It's Steven. How may I help you?" he replied.

"Steven. Good. I was wondering if I could uh... speak to the owner of this dealership?"

"Sure, but is there any problem?"

"Nah. No problem at all."

"Well then maybe I can help you? What kind of car are you looking for?"

"Uhh... a Chevy truck, or something from 02 on up. But uh... I'd also like to know how I could reach the owner."

"Sure. May I ask how come?"

This guy was beginning to get on my nerves. Question after question. Why couldn't he just get me the gottdamn owner for Fuck's sake?! I wasn't prepared for all this. I wasn't even sure what the hell I was doing. I was just playing by ear. "Yeah uhm, Steve. I've always wanted to see the owner in person."

"Well, sir. He's not in at the moment, but if you want I can show you to the manager."

"The manager. Ok."

I was then reintroduced to Vince.

"Hey, sup guy? What can I help you with? Everything Ok?" he asked.

"Yeah everything's cool. I know the car I want to get and everything, but I just wanted to know where I could find the owner."

"The Owner. You mean Mac. He's not in at the moment. How come?"

"I just wanted to know his name, so that I may thank him after I made my purchase."

I was just going off the top of my head now, though I knew it sounded weird. Vince kind of looked a bit confused, but then 'what-evere'd it.

"Tell you what buddy, let me set you up with Steve again, and then after you buy the car, you can write a 'thank you' letter. We'll make sure it gets to the boss ok?"

"Sure." I was getting nowhere. "Listen, Vince. Could you just tell me if ever and when the owner, Mac, gets in?"

"I couldn't tell you buddy. He comes in when he pleases."

"Oh ok." I ended up just walking out the door. That didn't go too smoothly, but at least I got the owner's nickname out of the ordeal. Now it was just a matter of figuring out the next move.

T was supposed to be with me on this assignment, but he kind of just strayed off. He said he had another task and that I should be able to handle it. I thought 'fine'. He seemed to be going through the motions lately anyway. Maybe it was good for him to take a break. So I'm really on my own with this one now. No big deal.

The next three days I spent being surveillant of the dealership. From 6 o'clock in the evening I would just arrive outside somewhere near the dealership, park my car and then wait. To help pass the time I'd listen to the radio, read the papers or take a step into the pizza restaurant, which was situated right across the street from the car lot, to play the arcade. Figure that I was doing a stakeout, only I've got nothing to go on but a nickname. I just kept a lookout for anyone I saw going in to the dealership for the night.

As one could imagine, I grew real impatient by my third night. Plus, this had to be done in a time frame of a little less than 2 weeks. So I decided that this would be my last night doing the stakeout. Surely, there had to be some other way of locating this guy. This stakeout just didn't seem as if it was going to workout fast enough.

Just then, at around 8:00pm, I get a tap on the passenger side window. It startled me, as it woke me up. "Hey you. Everything alright in there?" spoke the voice of the guy standing outside my car.

"Uhh... I rolled down the passenger window to communicate better. "Yeah. I'm just waiting for somebody." I couldn't really see the guy clearly. It was dark outside and I wasn't near a street lamp. On top of that, the man seemed to be bending over, but he wasn't low enough for me to see his face through the window.

"Yeah. Well sorry to disturb you."

"That's ok mister." I politely replied.

And with that, the guy walked away towards the corner behind my vehicle. I made sure to look through the rearview mirror to see if I could get a better glimpse of him. But I could only see the back of him. He wore a pear of jeans and a dark brown jacket. The only thing I could make out other than his wears was that he was a white guy. At first I thought to myself, 'Oh good. Now I can go back to my surveillance.' But then I immediately began to question why the man came to the car in the first place. Who was he? Why would he or anybody think that I'm in need of help? All sorts of other questions like this began to play in my head. I grew a little more cautious.

93

Around 40 minutes later I decided to pull out and
call it a night. But then, I saw a car roll up into the
dealership lot and disappear behind the gate. I'm thinking
that hopefully it's him. "Finally," I said to myself, as I
began to ease my chair up and figure my next move.
After a few extra moments of pondering I decided that I'd
just simply go up in there and act like I wanted to see a
car. I would insist on seeing the owner. And although the
dealership is long closed for the night – I'd just rely on the
fact that New York was full of idiots and I'd play one of
them.

So I began to load up. Then, again, I heard
another set of taps on the passenger side window.

'Tap-Tap-Tap'.

"Shit!" I exclaimed even more startled. I was now
even more on edge due to what I had in mind. I rolled
down the window in frustration and snapped out, "What?!
What d'ya want?!"

"Sorry sir. It's me again. The guy from earlier."

I still couldn't see this guys face. This minor
mystery, coupled with being startled twice in a row, began
to put me in a state of great annoyance. "Yeah! What is it
now?!"

"I'm just checking on you out of concern."

I opened the door and got out to face this guy. I
stood leaning on the roof of the drivers' side with the door
still opened. "Like I said earlier mister, whoever you are
to be concerned, I'm alright." I could see his face now.
He was a young looking white guy with dark hair and an
almost invisible scar on his brow. And now that I could
see his face he seemed to be verbalizing in contempt.

"Well. It's not me who's concerned. It's the
neighbors who are concerned. There's a report of a
strange vehicle and unrecognized person on their block."

"Yeah? So they sent you? What are you a cop?"

"Yes I am."

Oh no. I was thinking to myself, '*don't panic*'. So I'm
dealing with a cop. He's just like anybody else. I'll tone
down a little bit so as not to give cause for an altercation.
"Ok officer. Do you have a badge?"

"Well if I showed you that sir, then it would be
official. Then I'd have to actually care why you are here
and investigate. I'm just gonna point blank let you know
that I live on this block and there is to be no trouble. Not
assuming that there is, but quite frankly, if my neighbors
are concerned then I am concerned."

"Whoa Serpico. Why am I being here a concern
to the neighborhood? I'm no threat. It's cause' I'm
black?"

"No, it's cause your vehicle has been sitting here
off and on for 3 nights now. And I don't buy that shit
about waiting for your 'somebody' either. Now it's a free
country, but I'm warning you. You better not be here to
make trouble."

"No trouble officer. I wasn't aware that I was
frightening people. I'll leave."

Nothing more was said with that. I was just
relieved he didn't try to play Robocop. But then, who the
fuck did this fucko think he was muscling? How the hell
did I know if he was a real cop anyway? Fuck him. I
pulled off down the block and looked through my
rearview mirror as I saw him enter the pizza shop I was
frequenting for the past few days on my stakeout. I made
a U-Turn and then drove slowly passed the shop to peer
inside. In there, I saw him talking what looked like
something serious to a very concerned looking pizza man.
Could the pizza man be that concerned citizen? I was so
amused that I sped down the block, almost forgetting
about the dealership bit.

Time goes by and I decide to head back and park
somewhere more out sight where I couldn't be recognized.
As I'm nearing the dealership I could see two guys

through the glass door windows carrying on a discussion. I walked up and tapped on the glass.

"Hey. You guys. Can you help me?" They waved me away to motion that they were closed, but I just stood there like I couldn't understand.

After almost a minute of this, one of the two men, an older looking pepper-haired guy, finally came towards the glass window with an irate look. He yelled out through the glass that they were closed. Still, I played the fool and acted like I couldn't understand him. "Huh? I can't hear you! I need to buy a car!" He then opened the door in frustration, as if he couldn't wait to open it so that he could let me have a piece of his mind. Little did he know that I was intending to leave a piece of his mind all over the waxed dealership floor.

The door was halfway opened when the old man blurted out, "What're you an idiot? We're closed! Get outta here and come back tomorrow."

He then instantaneously attempted to close and relock the door, but I had already stuck my foot in between, followed by some aggressive pushing. "No. Please! I need to buy a car! And I need it tonight man! Na' mean?"

Then another guy came over to his assistance.

"What the fuck is going on? What's the fucking problem? We're closed. Ok? Don't make me have to say it again."

"Hey fuck you," I replied. "I want a car and I want a car now!"

"What the fuck did you just say to me?" He then yelled out towards the back. "Hey VINCE! BRING MY BAT!" He turned again towards me. "I'll teach you to mind your manners you cock sucker. Get the fuck outta here or I'll bash your brains in!"

I then spotted Vince emerging out the back with an iron pipe. 'Oh great' – I'm thinking to myself sarcastically.

"What's the problem Mac? This guy bothering you?" Challenges Vince, as he inches up towards where we were standing to get a better look at me. "Holy shit, that's the clown that kept asking for you earlier?"

He said it. The magic words – Mac! But although he seemed to be referring the name to the younger more hot-tempered guy, it seemed indirect. This young guy couldn't be the owner of all this. So I pushed my luck. "Wait. Which one of you is Mac? That's all I wanted… to buy a car from the owner."

"I'm Mac you idiot," the older looking gentlemen answered, as the other guy, who had threatened to assault me with the bat simultaneously advised Mac not to answer. Yep. This guy was the owner, just as I figured. He continued, "What the HELL can't you understand? Get the fuck outta here you moron before we call the police."

"The police?! Hey, sure thing, Mac!" I answered mockingly. "I'll be on my way, cause I'm a good guy and I don't want any trouble. But…" I then produced my pistol and continued. "…But my little black concealed friend here has something he wants to get out of his system.

"HOLY SHIT!!" yelled Vince as I instantly fired two shots point blank into Mac's forehead. BLA-BAM! - Went the semi-auto. The other two guys just stood there paralyzed in disbelief. Then Vince put both hands up and pleaded. "D-Don't shoot me man. I just work here!"

I complied with Vince's wish and fired instead, at the other loud mouth guy who threatened me with the bat before, as he made a dash for the back. I fired wildly at him, but he was moving like hot wheels and disappeared into the back office. I'm wondering to myself – *'did I get him? I think I got him.'* No time for speculation. I take one step towards where he retreated and was nearly stunned motionless when he emerged back out with a pistol of his own. "YOU MOTHER FUCKER!" he shouted, as he started firing wildly at me. I had no other faster option, but to jump behind one of the showroom cars sitting in its' lobby. I'm too nervous now to peek, in fear that my head might get blown off. So I stick my gun hand out instead and start firing in the direction I think he is. Now, it's a gunfight.

I'm firing only a few shots at a time, but the other guy is shooting like he's upset, letting off shots almost non-stop every time he sees me scurrying between the two cars. I started to get fed.

"DON'T THINK YOU'RE GONNA TRAP ME HERE YOU FUCK FACE! I'LL COME OVER THERE AND BLAST YOUR FUCKING HEAD OFF!" I yelled out in cockiness.

"C'MON THEN!" – POP goes his gun. "C'MON YOU COCSUCKER!" – POP goes his gun again. Then in a few volleys – POP… POP… POP POP.

Some of the bullets were crashing all the way through the doors and getting too close for comfort. I only grew more restless. Was this guy going to run out of bullets or what? I decided that I was going to just make a dash for the door, which were just a couple steps from me. I figured I would just jump up and 'Rambo' my way backwards, but when I looked; Vince was still by the doorway. The bullets stopped flying from both of us for a quick couple seconds.

"Yo! Get the FUCK outta the doorway!" I emphasized over.

But then the other guy continued to talk shit. "You stay right there Vince! You don't let this sonofabitch get passed ya!"

Vince Just stood there, still with the iron pipe in his hand.

"What's it gonna be Vince? I don't want to have to shoot you outta my way, but I will!"

"Fuck him Vince! You hold post. He starts coming towards ya I'll blow his fucking tail off!"

That seemed to have reinforced Vince's confidence, for he looked as though his mind was made up to hold the fort indeed. He grabbed the iron pipe now with both hands and almost dared me to get passed him.

"C'mon you mother fucker and I'll kn-knock your fucking block off."

Very daring. And I really didn't want to shoot him, but he was leaving me no options.

Then the other guy started again. "Fuck that. I'm coming through."

And I believed he was coming too, so I pulled a 'fuck it' move of my own. As the other gunman began to emerge from his spot and approach boldly towards my area, I bum rushed Vince, crashing both of us through the glass windows. I almost simultaneously bounced back up to make a dash for it, but a gruesome sight lay before me. Vince, through the impact of the crash, had a large piece of glass sticking through his back. He started to gasp out blood as he wriggled around on the ground, trying to make sense of the pain he was feeling. I stared in disbelief. I didn't plan for this to happen. True I didn't really know Vince from a hole in the wall, but this was the first time I have caused something to happen to someone of that grotesque nature, for whom I didn't mean it to happen to.

In the brief two seconds that I looked down at him in a sort of new shock, I wanted to apologize. Of course though, I had no time. The gunman was coming out with a vengeance, so I continued to hurriedly make my way out the dealership lot. Then, it was evident that he saw the state of Vince in the way he wailed out new obscenities. It almost sounded like he was just plain crying. He chased me no more.

Whilst in flight, as I took a quick glance back over my shoulder, I could see him kneeling next to his partner, looking as though he was trying to figure out what he could do. I don't know why, but I felt very bad about that for some time.

As I casually made my way back across the street towards my car as if nothing happened, I see that same guy whom earlier identified himself as the concerned civil servant. Only now, there was no question of whether he was really a cop or not, cause he was approaching me with his gun drawn and his badge on his belt.

"Police! Drop the weapon! Drop the fucking weapon!" he ordered.

"Ok! Don't shoot!" I requested, as I put one hand in the air and lowered, as though I was placing the gun on the ground.

"I said DROP it! DROP the weapon!" He moved forward with the gun still fixed on me.

"Sorry! Don't shoot me I'm listening." I dropped the gun on the pavement. While he was shouting the usual orders, I decided I'd have to pull something. He was going to have to shoot me. I don't do incarceration. I attempted a desperate trick and I still marvel at how it worked in the first place.

He was still only halfway between my car and me across the street. He shouted the next order that I very well followed. At the same time, I had glanced behind him towards my car and had mouthed a pretense. This was to create the illusion that I might've had an accomplice behind him. Psychology. I just needed him to flinch once. Naturally he feared something might be up and wanted to take no chances with his life. With the gun still on me, he took a split-second glance over his shoulder. Something I'm sure they didn't suggest for him to do at the academy. Aware that my gun was still only two feet away from when he ordered me to back away from it; I made a dash for it with what only the almighty must've granted to me as the perfect timing. It only took a split second for me to grab my gun firing. And how we didn't hit each other at that moment was just another marvel of the gun.

We both ran for our respective covers. He taking shield by my vehicle and me taking shield behind the only other car parked a couple feet to my right. Thank goodness it was there. I know it wasn't when I first entered the lot. Still, I couldn't fully count my blessings yet. The off-duty officer was holding fort with my car, and I knew it was a matter of time before more like him would show. I either had to blast my way towards him and re-take control of my vehicle, or run. I felt that my odds were better if I shoot my way back.

There was a brief cease-fire while we were both taking cover. I guess he figured he needn't have to shoot as long as back up would be arriving shortly and I kept at bay. At least that's how I figured it. Out of all those gunshots, somebody had to call the police. With no more hesitation, I pulled another fuck-it move and broke the cease of fire.

"COME OUT WITH YOUR HANDS UP!" the off-duty hero yelled out.

"SURE." With both hands on the gun, I jumped up and started firing at him through my car. I could see that he returned fire, yet still he was trying to hide and shield himself from the barrage. This gave me the confidence to push it. I started walking towards the car, firing steadily now with one hand, while readying another clip. It was only a brief couple seconds from then did I realize that he wasn't returning fire. I paused for a moment. Why wasn't he shooting back? This could be a trap, but I knew I didn't have time to speculate, so I continued over to the car with my finger ever so ready on the trigger. "C'mon muthaphucka. I'm ready for ya." There was still no response even when I got to my car. With my heart pounding heavily, my gun and I slowly peeked around to where the cop was. There he was alright, slumped over as if he was just too tired. Only, he was barely moving. I aimed my gun for his head. "Hey! This is no time to be playing possum." Still he crouched there with little to no motion. I slowly used my foot to push him back, and he fell backwards staring around in impaired orientation. I hadn't noticed before that there was blood all in front of him and on my rear passenger side door. "Oh shit," I said, well surprised of the outcome.

At a close street examination, I found at least two bullet wounds. There was one that grazed his head and another in his shoulder bone. He would live. How such sure hits when he was hiding behind my car all the while? I examined my car and saw a few bullet holes projecting outwards, towards where he would be hiding. I glanced back down at the officer. 'They just don't make cars like they used to,' I thought to myself. From off of him I took only his service pistol and left his badge and wallet. I jumped in my car and sped off, before the sound of a siren. All of what just took place happened faster than what thought. My conscious did bother me about Vince and the cop. Both of them were unintended victims. I found it easy to dispatch of contracted targets, mainly because I knew that they were soulless and in the game; much like myself. But for all of this that happened tonight. There were more victims than needed. One innocent bystander, to my knowledge and an officer of the law. This was sloppy. At least the cop would live. That fact helped me cope with my conscious better.

***

And then it hit me… The cop saw my face; the other gunman in the dealership saw my face; the pizza man in the shop saw my face. I'm pretty sure that between the pizza man and the cop, the vehicle that I was using has been compromised by description. Panic was beginning to set in again. That warm fuzzy feeling in my chest. It was decided by me, that I was not going to try and take out the witnesses. Wasting time to take out the

other gunman from the dealership would be just that; a
waste of time. There was still the cop and the pizza man.
Taking out the cop was out of the question. And the pizza
man? I just couldn't. I wanted no more innocent
bystanders.

At this point... it could not go well for me.

Chapter VI – A slight shift in Power

Immediately after my last job, I decided that it was time for a vacation. I've put in too many man executing hours and had not received the appropriate amount of time off I felt I deserved. I knew it wasn't a matter of if I could take off, but rather only a question of when and how long. There was no real leader of our crew for a while since Grip was killed. Only my cousin Trevor seemed suitable enough to take control and run things. All the other guys were just there. The few guys that were there before T were dead, incarcerated or just disappeared. So me being T's cousin made me feel kind of greatly about myself. If the only person I had to answer to was T, well then who's stopping me from doing what I wanted? I felt I had a little pull. It was evident that a few things had indeed changed since the passed few years of my induction. And still, a few more things were about to change.

I walked into our bar/headquarters to get a drink, mellow out and possibly meet up with T. It was Friday night, so I expected a good turnout. Upon entering the bar I was greeted by all the regulars. The lights were dim as usual and the Smoke filled air was a mix of both cigarettes and weed. A live performance on the stage by some blues band kept the scene mellow, just the way I liked things. And the customers, who were a little more than usual, seemed to be digging it. A few of the crewmembers were here and there, and we nodded to each other in recognition upon sight. My man Pipe, the man who executed the street drug czar Richie with me, was there at the bar carrying on a conversation with the bar help. When he looked over in my direction I assumed he had seen me smile and give him the nod, but I guess he didn't. He just turned back to finish his conversation with the bartender, without any acknowledgement of me whatsoever.

As I'm contemplating whether to make my way over there, I see her come in. It was Grip's ex again. She walked into the bar, followed by a familiar cat. I realized then that it was some other dude from one of the other bars. He was an associate friendly whom I've seen around once or twice; nobody really important. I watched as he checked their coats and led her to a table. 'Gottdamn those curves', I thought to myself. The tight black dress she was wearing revealed solid goodness. Of course I wanted to at least catch her eye, but then I quickly decided against it. I mean, the first encounter almost brought about a fight, and the second encounter she just plain took my offered proposal and never once called. Fuck that. There would not be a strike three with me. I'd rather just leave it alone. I quickly turned my head from her direction before she could notice me looking. I just continued over to the bar where Pipe was to grab a drink.

"Sup bud?" I greeted the bartender. "Let me get a beer". He popped open the brew and slid it a few feet across the table into my hand. "Thanks bud". I took a quick chug and turned on the swivel stool to face the performance. I knew Pipe was still right on the stool next to me on my left, but I waited for a half minute before saying anything.
Right after about the second chug, I attempted to start small talk.

"Sup P? How's it going?" I asked, not even bothering to face him.

"Chillin," he answered in his usual low tone, with his back facing the performance. He was still facing the bar. I could tell he didn't bother to turn his head either.

"Yep." I only smiled to myself. I suppose one could just take it as Pipe just being himself. At least that's what I suggested to myself to clear my mind of conflict. Deep down though, from those few scenarios that evening, I could tell he had a problem with me. For what, I knew not. But I didn't dwell on it much. I was more concerned with Grip's ex; whom I felt by now should've been mine. Instead, she's over there cheesing away with some cornball. I ordered another drink and just sat there on the stool facing the performance. Rather, pretending to be into the performance, while glancing in their direction moments at a time.

So I'm just sitting there and keeping a low profile, when who should walk in, but Carla-LaTina. The quiet one from the Tina sisters that T introduced to me a while back, she was very beautiful. She too had a bad dress with a killer body and even a little more shapelier than Grip's ex. My attention was %100 shifted from Grip's ex to her now, as she glided across the room, socializing with some of the regulars. I decided that it was time for a now bolder me to approach.

I grabbed a few mints out of the bar cup so as to rid the stench of alcohol from my breath. I then excused myself from the bar and made my way over to the crowd where she was. My goal was to pretend that my true intentions were to mingle with the crew, rather than her. It worked.

"Sup fellas?" I asked, as I greeted the crew, pretending that I didn't see Carla. "What's the word?"

"Everything is everything guy," one of them replied. "Sup with you? T told us about you and that thing? I..."

"Yeah, the thing," I cut him off, getting the feeling that I knew what he was going to mention. "Serious business. But say, have you seen T?" It might have seemed rude to just cut him off like that, but hey. He was referring to my last job, which I didn't even want to remember myself. He should've known better than to bring up these things in public anyway. No matter how well you try to disguise it, it still should rarely ever be discussed outside the circle.

At first I thought he picked up on the hint, but he instead continued to go on half-wittedly about everything that wasn't wise to say amidst our surroundings. "Ayo. Ayo Non, how that thing went down man? I'm saying... That shit was serious. That could've put us out of commission on the real!"

By now, I'm quite annoyed with this guy. What the fuck was he doing? He now had a few of the women in the group pestering him as to what the big secret was, while a few members from our team looked on in amusement. I'm now upset about two things. For one, this clown was talking out of his mouth in an open area. And then second, the few guys in our own crew didn't even make an effort to help me curb the guy. I guess they figured that since they had nothing to do with it, then it wasn't a big deal. Just let me handle it. Amazing. However, I could tell that this talking moron had a little too much to drink. That, or he just wanted to impress his surroundings; or both.

"Look... um... brotha..." I began. I really didn't know his name. All I knew was that he was an affiliate that transferred over here through the approval of the crew. Approval or not though, it was time for me to put him in check. I continued, "We can't talk about this right now, nah mean? The people. But yo, later on I gotta fill you in on that, k?" I didn't want to down play him in front of the people, so I tried to sound as polite as possible. I thought that would get through his inebriated skull with no more problems. However, it only made things escalate further somehow.

"Aint no thing brotha, if that's what we calling each other now. Nah mean?" He turned to the guys jokingly, whom only grinned back. "I'm saying... the man said chill right? So i'ma chill. Still though, a nigga could know a nigga name and all."

'Oh oh' is all I could think towards that response. It was one of those non-laudable responses that easily turned minor things into major disputes. Where was this coming from? I knew that he must've had a few drinks, but c'mon. On top of that, the guys still weren't backing me. Just waiting to see what it turned into. Amusing still, yet I knew I should just play it cool.

"Sorry man. N..." I began, only to have him cut me off abruptly.

"It's Mann chief. Short for Manuel."

"Ok Mann. Not a thing." I continued. At this phase, I was already doing a miraculous job of containing my temper. "I'm out fellas. Let T know I was looking for him please."

Then Carla intervened. "Trevor? Hey, I'm looking for him too."

I turned to face the source of the sweet voice. In the brief and uneasy dialogue I had with that clown Mann, I almost forgot about Carla, who was my reason for coming there in the first place.

"Hey," I smiled warmly. "I remember you? How are you?"

"I'm fine," she replied, with a cute smile all her own. "I remember you as well. How have you been?"

"I'm chillin. Just taking in the evening here amongst friends," I answered, half sarcastically. "Say, you wanna go find a table and sit down with me? That way you can rest your legs, we can chat and look out for my cousin at the same time."

"I'd love to," she replied. And the way she responded with that pretty smile, I just knew that she had to be attracted to me.

So off Carla and I were set to go. I again bade the crew adieu and took Carla by her soft silky hand to make our way to a table. I felt very good about myself now, for I saw, came and seized the moment. Yet, my mental hiatus quickly went when Mann made still another comment.

"Peace out Nigga! I hope you don't forget shortie name before the night is up!" He joked, followed by a few chuckles from the crew.

Unbelievable. He was really asking for it. Clever him putting it in the form of a joke, but I got the message. He was trying to clown me. People outside the crew might just see it as a friendly joke, while the noise from the band made it so that no one else in the area might've even cared to hear. But the guys in the crew, they heard it. This guy was testing me in front of the crew and I knew that's just how it had to come across to them.

I was very infuriated inside now by this comedian. I had an image to maintain. Ever since T had assumed authority of the crew I couldn't help but feel that I had some authority myself. Now here comes this no-name clown from out of the blue trying to undermine me. It was only because I was already on my way to the table with Carla that I didn't choose to say anymore on that. I only put up my hand to gesture that I had accepted the joke in good humor and give up. In actuality though, I was itching to put a hot one right in his medulla oblongata.

So now I'm just chilling there with this fine lady. And a lady she was. Every characteristic about her spelled class. She wasn't stuck up either. She knew she was an attractive lady, but didn't play on that. She was just chill. She could hang with the fellas', but knew her role as a woman. She knew how to act. She knew her place.

We talked of all sorts of shit. We talked about the past, the present and the future. We talked about back in da' days and Saturday morning cartoons. We talked about everything from current world events, to the sun, the moon and the stars. It was when we started talking about morality that I grew a bit uneasy.

"So how long have you and Trevor been close?" she asked, quite innocently.

"Oh me and Ts been cool since the sandbox days. Overtime he had to move so we kind of lost contact like we used to. But the feeling of brotherhood between us has always been."

"You speak pretty fondly of your cousin. That's cool. I think it's a good idea that all family members should have that bond, especially in these days. You know, the world can be a very cruel place when you're down, out and have no one to turn to."

"Ha. Hmpf. Tell me about it. T-e-l-l ME about it. I was there man. I was there. Did you know at one point I was homeless? I couldn't even take refuge in a shelter. And then, just when I thought that the almighty felt I had enough abuse, I nearly get killed by some two-bit bum! You know? It's a miracle that..." I had to stop myself. Not only was I getting a bit carried away, but I was revealing too much of myself. She just seemed so cool that I felt I knew her personally for years. "It's just a miracle that my cousin Trevor rescued me when he did. And for that, I love him."

"Wow. I... I don't even know what to say." She reached over and put her soft gentle hand on my forearm. "I can't even imagine what a frustrating ordeal you had to go through, and I'm sure that there's so much more to the story, but let's just thank the almighty creator that you're alright. I mean, you can't be too hard on him, he did lead you to Trevor." She glowed with a pleasant smile. Her eyes were that of a pure look of concern.

"I guess so." I smiled to myself, looking down as though a shy youth. I looked into her eyes again momentarily, and then quickly reverted back to her response. I didn't want to fall for her, nor her fall for me; there was just something about her that seemed too sweet and pleasant. "So you're a Christian woman huh?"

"Well... not so much of a Christian as a spiritualist."

"What's the main difference?" I don't know if she found my ignorance to religion pitiful or refreshing, but she didn't hesitate to enlighten me.

"Well Christianity is basically a religion, derived from Jesus Christ and based on the bible as sacred scripture. Spirituality is more so just the sensitivities towards religious values. At least that's how I see it".

"Hmm. Interesting. Well you seem a very spiritual woman. I mean I've got to be honest with you when I say that I feel drawn to you. You have a warmness about you."

"Aww. You must say that too all the pretty girls." We both laughed.

"Nah. Just you."

There was another moment of pause and then she continued, "So do you ever feel that the trials & tribulations from your past affect your present life?"

"What? Uh, nah not really. I mean, I just keep my head up and do what I do." She had caught me off guard.

"So what do you do? Do you do what T does?"

"And, what would T do?"

"I'm asking you?"

"I roll with T. Yeah."

"Hmpf. I see."

"What? What's the problem?"

"Well, you do know what T does right? I don't think I have to tell you what the problem is if you roll with him."

"Carla, where is this coming from?"

"I'm sorry. It's just my observation. I mean I know I've only known you briefly, but I think you're a real cool person. And quite honestly, I feel very drawn to you as well. It's just that, I don't know how deep you are into your profession with T."

"I see. Well... I do what I do, because it's the only acceptable way I can make a decent living on my own terms. I did begin doing what I did, because T showed me the way. Without him I'd probably be homeless or dead. So, some of these seemingly monstrous acts that I must perform are just the shit that comes with the job. It's just a part of me."

"Well, I worry about that. I've always worried about Trevor like a brother and I'm worried about you now. I mean, I wouldn't consider selling marijuana a monstrous act, but there are dangers involved in the distribution of any narcotics."

"Marijuana?" I almost sounded amused.

"Yeah. Mary Jane. You don't have to hide it, Trevor told me everything. Unless, you're selling other things too."

"Uhh..." I couldn't even respond right away. I was still amused at the fact that through all this time, she thought it was just drugs; and Marijuana at that. It was very humorous and I was tickled on the inside. I was just trying hard not to show it.

She continued, "Well, I'm not that naive to believe its just marijuana, I'm sure it's other narcotics."

"Really?" I started to chuckle to myself.

"What's so funny? This is serious."

"I'm... I'm sorry Carla," I apologized, while desperately trying to suppress growing inner laughter.

"Whatever. I'm just saying. You seem sweet and Trevor is like a brother, I guess to both of us. I know y'all do your dirt, but there are worst things out there. At least you guys don't go around robbing banks or taking people's lives. Hell, that's the worst thing anybody can do."

"What... uhm... robbing banks?" I asked, now with the chuckling and inner laughter fading.

"No silly. Taking people's lives. That is the worst."

"You don't say."

"But I don't worry, cause those monsters always get their 'just desserts' anyway."

"Hm. I hear you." My whole feeling of humor had by now turned into self-pity.

"Hey, but don't look so down kiddo. You and Trevor will be all right. I know sometimes people go through trying periods and sometimes they just got to sell a little, just till' they get back on their feet. Just saying, please, don't let your past be the reason for the demise of your future."

The rest of that evening we talked about other things, drank and slow danced the night away. That night at the bar was indeed pleasant. True that at some point during our recent discussion I suffered a serious guilt trip. But as the night went on I had forgotten about it. She was such an innocent; at least compared to most. This was a definite attraction.

Much later on that night, about 30 minutes to closing time, T came in. Without so much as greeting anyone, but the few already in the doorway, he quickly descended his way down into the cellar basement. By now, most the customers had already left, so it was just myself, Carla, the rest of the crew and a few of their outside company. The band was packing up and there was small talk amongst all the few that remained. I don't believe Carla even noticed that T already came about, as he did disappear as suddenly as he showed up. She excused herself to the restroom and I waited patiently in my seat. I was again admiring her body as she made her way to the restroom, but at the same time wondered if all was all right with T. It wasn't unusual for him to come through late, but the hurriedness of his arrival seemed urgent. By the time Carla came back out, I was up taking a stretch.

"What's up? Got tired of waiting?" she joked.

"Nah. Just saw your boy Trevor come in and wanted to see what's up."

"He came?! When?!"

"Oh about 15 minutes ago. He went down the back."

"Wha... and you didn't tell me?" she gasped.

"Well, nah. It's only been 15 minutes."

"Aww, shame on you. You know I was waiting for him." she smiled.

"Well c'mon. We can check him together."

We made our way towards the back and were going to continue down into the cellar, until Keith, the 6'4 270lb bouncer, blocked us. He was nicknamed 'Keith the Guerilla'. Not the monkey. He wasn't someone to monkey around with. We called him Guerilla, because he looked like a one-man militia, in size and appearance. He wasn't an official member of the crew or anything, just hired help. We respected and trusted him, so he knew what we were basically about by now. Just not in details.

"Sorry. She can't come trough here," stated Keith, in a very heavy and authorative voice.

I didn't take it personal. He just genuinely always sounded like that.

"Why not Keith?"

"Orders of T. You can come through, of course, but no one other than the regulars."

"Aww. You sure?" asked Carla. "I'm a longtime friend of his and I'm sure he'd have wanted to see me."

"Sorry ma'am. No exceptions." The guerilla then turned to me and gave a look of surety. "Crew only."

I knew it was of importance, so I ended up walking Carla back to her car. She was a bit upset that she didn't get to see T, but I assured her that I would let him know she came through and that I'd call her and let her know everything's alright. After a little more brief talk, I thanked her for the evening, gave her the ole' hug & kiss and then headed back to the bar.

So now the crew and I are gathered in the bar basement, which we deemed the base for obvious reasons, for a meeting called to order by T. It was a well-lit and roomy area. Almost like a miniature office floor without the desk and computers. I, along with everyone else, was wondering exactly what this surprise meeting was about. Everyone, for the most part, knew that when there was a meeting in the basement, it was most likely to discuss hush-hush events of sorts. Or issues on anything from robbery, to murder, to planned events and even gripes within the crew. So I figured that either the meeting was a gripe that maybe some crewmember had with me, or the botched thing with the mob hit. But, nothing prepared me for what the true intent of the meeting was for.

I'm there just looking around and I see all the familiars, except for T. I also notice a few members from the other Org affiliated jurisdictions, including the guy that Grip's ex walked into the bar with earlier. This was a first. Usually, meetings in the base only meant the regulars, so that not even other affiliates were allowed. Every group usually respectively had their own meetings. Then an ambassador of sorts, or crew leaders themselves, would have a meeting with each other if warranted. But at the time I just guessed that T knew what he was doing. There were only like five of them anyway, which altogether totaled about 27 of us in that room.

Ok. All were there, but where was T? Pretty soon, the chatter amongst everyone grew, as some started to grow impatient. The only guys who weren't talking were I, Pipe and some other guy. Then shortly after, in comes T with Keith the Guerilla; yet another amusing thing to myself and I'm sure others. Absolutely no bar help allowed in the base. Yet, here was T making his way towards the middle of the base floor with the bouncer.

"Night fellas," T began. Everyone grew silent. "Thanks all for showing up tonight and pardon my lateness. I guess you're all wondering why I gathered you all here tonight."

"I know. You're bout to carry out a hit on all of us," one member joked from the audience, followed by roars of laughter from everyone else. Even T.

"Nah, no. I'm not gonna' whack you guys," mocked T, in a makeshift Italian accent. "I just wanna talk to yuz."

Soon a few of the members were heckling and goofing around, like trying to rush T to get on with it. So I myself interjected, "Go ahead T. We're listening."

"Well," he continued, now in a stern manner, "I guess you can say I'm what you call a 'made-man'."

"Say what?" was the feedback from a few. Everyone else was just silent.

T continued, "I just became Kinged' today. Totally unexpected, but it was what they felt was appropriate." He then humored, "No arguments from me."

At first the room remained silent, then after a few 'are you serious' type inquiries, and verification from the other bosses in the room, there was applause. This is why T wanted a few of the other major affiliates and their bosses there. So he can announce this and make it official. The headmen were obviously present or notified by a true 'Org rep' as to T's induction. If not, then I were sure there would have been a lot of 'sez who's' and confusion that night. But it was all set. This all came as a shock to me just as anyone else, but of course I was happy for him. This meant he was officially the boss of our crew. No more sideline mumbling as to who should really run the outfit among our crew. It was set in stone. Anyone not an actual Org made boss who challenged that, including myself, was not fit and would be lethally punished. But what would I have to worry about? I figured T's new promotion would only be positive for me. And then, it happened.

"Oh. I have one more announcement," began T again. The room grew silent once more. "Guerilla!"

Keith 'the guerilla' makes his way from the door, where he's been standing the whole time and approaches the guy that Grip's ex was escorted by earlier. Before the escort could even ask, "What the fu -?" Pipe and another guy grabs him from both sides and forces him down to his knees before Keith. "What the fuck? What the fu - What the fuck is going on?!" is all this guy kept asking, the pitch in his voice obviously that of fear and confusion.

"I think you guys should back away, it's about to get messy," suggests T, as he lights a blunt he had pulled out from his shirt pocket.

The audience backs up in wonder and confusion as the guerilla pulls out a .9mm semi-auto and points it straight at the escort's forehead. "Any Last words?" he asks. The only thing the escort could ask, or repeat, was 'what the fuck'. And with that, the guerilla looks up at T, from whom he gets the nod, and squeezes a hot slug neatly into the center of the escort's forehead.

Everyone is stunned and just staring, some even in horror at the randomness of it. But T assured the room that it wasn't random at all. He goes on to explain that the guy was an informant and tried to start his own operations. He then went on to explain the rules of what we do.

After all this, Pipe and the other guy who held the escort down began to clean up as T, abruptly wishes everyone a good evening and retires out of sight. Everyone is sort of hurrying out and muttering to themselves on what just happened. I myself couldn't believe it. Everything coupled into one - the announcement by T, the execution of the guy before everyone, the execution being executed by the help. It was all too much. And at the end T was once again nowhere to be found that night.

Later on I found out that the escort was setup by whom he was escorting; Grip's ex. If that didn't blow me away enough, the bar help was now a crewmember. Well I guess that should've been obvious after what he just done, but still. I figured out the whole thing. T not only wanted to let everyone know he was the boss, but he wanted to instill the fear of harsh discipline to the others. The way he set it up was perfect now that I think about it. Pretty sadistic. See, you've got a room of hardened killers, so how do you get them to respect, if not fear, your authority? Simple. You punish one of them. And not only do you punish him, but orchestrate his punishment as something random. Something sudden. Something that sends out the impression that it could've been anyone of us with the back of our heads plopped on the floor. Then you disappear as suddenly as you came in, leaving the room to wonder... 'What the fuck just took place here? This guy is crazy!' Yeah, T played this whole thing out right. But now, I even found myself mindful of T from time to time and suddenly I didn't like that. I didn't like where this thing seemed it was heading.

***

Quickly after that it was business as usual. Trevor was in control, but he didn't fully play that card out - yet. All was normal and things were unusually quiet for a while. I felt it was all for a better piece of mind. My conscious was beginning to take on phase three of the guilty complex and I was constantly at unease, so I welcomed the calm. No big jobs. Just pick ups, drop offs and easy money. I was seeing Carla more often than usual nowadays, which did wonders for calming my anxieties; and all was mellow. As can be imagined, this was all good for the nerves. Just a Mecca of slow days and Carla. Naturally, that Mecca would be brief for me. My comfort zone would be cut short by a series of incidents beginning with one. Not that one necessarily had anything to do with the other, but it all re-triggered the monster in me.

Here I am in my zone for a couple of months now and about two jobs come up. Both hits. Both related

118

cases. I go along on both. There's usually always a clean-up man, but not these rounds. I didn't know when was the last time I cleaned up after the dead guy, until then. After that, nothing for a while again. T was rarely around as he used to, so he relayed his orders through me. Ya know - Pick up this package; drop off this load; pay so & so a visit cause their coming up short; etc. I evened out these tasks fairly. At least I felt so. Hell, I even did some myself. Long and short of the story is that there's talk amongst the crew of me 'thinking' I'm the boss and being T's favorite pet. I find this out through the bar help, which surprised me, cause I always felt like I was getting the 'shoulder vibe' from him as well. Perhaps it was just me. Go figure. But he reveals this to me nonetheless and even tells me who's behind it. Fucking Pipe. So I call a meeting with the crew late night in the basement and they all attend except T.

"Sup fellas. Glad you came through." They greeted me back in a manner of respect that I didn't expect. As if since I called the meeting they're all ears. "I called this brief meeting cause I had to sit back and ask myself if there were any issues within us that we need to discuss." The room remained silent. I continued, "Anything at all - whether it be the bar, life... me. Problems with *anything*, except the boss of course." I chuckled along with the crew on that one. Still no answers, yet the reception felt warm, so I figured all was cool. And for the most part it was, but of course there's always that one. "Well folks, I'm glad of the job you're all doing. I just wanted to make sure all is cool between us. So if there are no issues of importance to be put on the floor, then how was that game the other night?" I humored, followed by a few more chuckles, as well as non-related replies from the crew. Cool.

"Well yeah, who made you boss?" shot Pipe, sarcastically and out of the blue.

118

"Say what?" I turned towards the agitator and responded. The room quickly grew silent again.

"Ya heard. Who made you boss?"

"You think I'm the boss Pipe? I never said I was boss." I turn towards the rest of the crew, "You guys think I'm the boss?" The floors response was of 'not at all'. They countered that I was one of the coolest guys they knew. Only two didn't bother to respond and remained screw faced. I watched them closely. Pipe and Mann - the clown who had a few jokes previous when in the presence of Carla. They stood out in my mind the most. It was then that I realized that it wasn't the crew that had a problem, it was just them. They were trying to provoke something and up to now I don't know why.

"Man yall niggas frontin," Pipe relayed to the rest. "That's aight though. I know my position and I stand 'behine-it'. You trying to run shit 'onna' low cause T isn't around. I just know it."

"Oh you just know it huh?" I could feel my blood already start to boil. This guy was fucking wordless since I first met him. Now he had all these opinions. "I assure you Pipe. I assure you all. I'm not trying to be boss."

"Yeah? How do we know that?"

"What the... what the fuck is you talking about really?" I felt I just had it with this clown. "Where do you get off and why are you trying to hit me with this garbage?"

"I know what I'm 'talkingbout.'"

"Man. All I can tell you Pipe is to curb your Jealousy."

"WHAT?! WHAT?!" Pipe started to grow excited. "WHAT'CHU 'TALKINGBOUT' MAN?!"

Now I knew I had struck a nerve, but I wasn't in the mood to get into a yelling match. The other clown from earlier, Mann, didn't say a word the whole time, but I could still sense he was for Pipe in opposing me. I just stared back at the both of them, as Pipe was unloading two minutes of all sorts of irrelevant foolery. The type of foolish talk that contains enough clues of animosity yet has no real credence on the matter of why.

"Look, Pipe," I interrupted, somewhere in between whatever he was talking about. "I don't get neither you nor your point, but get this. I've listened to you raise your voice at me and explain nothing, but irrelevant bullshit for the past two minutes. All your 'hat-o-rade' is coming at me in the form of questions that you should already know the answer to. Nobody else has a problem with me, but you. Work it out."

And with that I just left the room. There was just no way I could engage in any conversation with this man without blowing up, and that wouldn't be good. I left without adjourning the meeting, but I'm sure the crew understood.

So on and so on. I get a call one day at my domain.

"Hello? I'm calling for Non?"

"Only Non at this number. Speaking."

"Hi. It's me."

"Who?"

"Sonja. Grip's ex." She giggles on the other line.

"Oh. Ha. Ha." I laughed, tone instantly switching to accommodation mode. "What a surprise. How are you?"

"I'm good. Just wanted to touch base with you, being that I never really called."

"Well. Never too late with me."

"So how come you never invited me over to your place yet?"

Now I'm thinking to myself, 'what game is this? She knows well that the number I gave her to my rest was the only way of us communicating again.' However, now she was playing Alzheimer's. I suspected that it was because she saw me getting all close and personal to Carla. Women. But I play into it anyway.

"I'm sorry. I guess I just couldn't reach you," I replied.

"Oh you guess huh? Well you can make it up to me by taking me out some night this week," she countered.

"No doubt."

The rest of the conversation went brief. Little talk about how things were going in each other's lives is how most the rest of it went. We planned to kick it this Friday night.

Sometime before then, I paid a surprise visit to cousin T. I know he didn't really appreciate surprise visits from any member of the business, but I figured 'what the hell'. It's hard to catch up with him anywhere else lately.

'Knock – Knock', I knocked.

"Who's there?" he asked from the other end, after a minute or two.

"Hac'm," I replied, in a disguised voice.

There was a quick pause before he continued to entertain the charade. "I don't know no Hac'm."

"Nigga you're supposed to say Hac'm who"

Another pause before he answers, "What?"

"Nigga Hac'm you don't see if I'm alive now and then?" I answered, undisguising my voice.

Without a word he unlocked the door and then opened slowly. When he realized for sure it was me, he waved me in and re-bolted the door behind him. He then produced a .45 semi-automatic handgun from behind his back and threw it on the couch, before plopping down next to it himself. I just sat on the other couch adjacent to him and observed him for awhile, while he just looked down at the floor with this hands clasped together in a praying fashion.

"Nigga are you praying?" I inquired jokingly.

"No. I was sleeping peacefully and you just disturbed it," he answered back irritably.

"My bad man," I apologized.

"And another thing. Cut calling me Nigga."

"Wha – why come?"

"Just cut it that's all."

"I'm saying T, alright. It just sounds like you offended by that all of a sudden. As if we wasn't calling each other that for a minute now."

"I'm not offended. It's just that other crew members might be."

"Say what?"

"Look," he began to sound even more impatient. "We can't be all buddy-buddy and shit anymore. Know what I'm saying? I mean we're still family and all me and you. But I got a shit load of responsibilities you can't imagine right now. Nah mean? I got shit I need to stay on top of. I got new shit I better stay on top of. And now that I'm officially running shit at the bar, I got to make sure there's harmony among the crew. I've got to show that I'm not playing favorites or none of that. I need to be good with everything and everything needs to be good with me. Basically, that's it. So, I know a nigga been hard to reach lately, I just don't want you to take that shit personal."

"Oh uh... Nah. I mean. I'm... I'm good," I replied. I was at a loss for words really. I mean, I guess I knew where he was coming from. But the whole shit tonight seemed choreographed, as if expecting me to approach him on it. I suppose common sense would have one see it coming, but this was T. Little by little I was seeing him change in a brief period of time. And there would be more changes.

"So you got me up now man. What's good?" T inquired.

"Well man, nothing really. Other than checking up on you, all is ok. Little shit here and there about me thinking I'm the boss circulating around the bar, but I guess you must've heard about that already."

123

"Exactly, that's the shit I don't want to think about."

"I understand that T. So, I'll chill on the buddy-buddy shit then. But I held a meeting on it. And…"

"You held a meeting?" T interrupted. "I didn't know about no meeting."

"Chill. It wasn't business. Shit was circulating around the crew about me and I wanted to get it straight. It was handled."

"Anything that has to do with the crew is business." He pondered to himself for a moment. "Continue."

"Well uh… I find the crew is ok. In my opinion, it's just one or two knuckleheads. You know. I'm relaying shit you want done and they're taking it as I'm trying to run things."

"Who?"

"Pipe. I'm not sure about the other one, but I think he's got hate in his blood too."

"Ok. I'll look into it. For now though, don't worry about relaying anything for me. I'll just do it myself. You know, to reduce friction."

"Oh ok."

His pager goes off and he excuses himself into the kitchen. I'm just sitting there in the room, and all of a sudden I realized that I don't even feel comfortable enough around him to turn on the television. So I'm just sitting there staring at a blank screen. Ten minutes later he comes back in.

"Yo, you straight?" he inquires.

"Yeah. I'm good. Just thinking about something."

"Well yo, I know it's been short and I hate to rush you out, but I got to take care of something."

"No problem T. I'll catch you at the bar."

"No problem Non," he replied as he walked me towards the door. As I'm making my way off the porch he added in humor, "And don't be showing up unannounced."

I only laughed it off, but I knew he was serious. And just as promised, T did excuse me from relaying his duties just as he suggested. Only he still didn't relay them himself. He just simply got someone else from the crew to do it. Me, I was pissed at first, but then relieved that the pressure of having the crew think I'm boss should at least ease. Funny thing though, this new relay guy was doing the exact same thing I was doing; yet I didn't hear Pipe run his mouth about that.

***

The Friday that I was supposed to go out with Sonja came and passed, but we didn't go out. I just kind of blew it off. I just felt like 'why'? All I know is that she blew me off when I expected to go out with her a stretch ago. Now I'm with Carla and she's interested. Nah, not me. I haven't the time. Besides, I did have Carla now. And Carla had me. It was sweet too. We did all the fancy, yet affordable stuff couples do when they first meet each other. We went to dinners, but at bar & grills. We took trips to the Pocono mountains; Disney world; and a cruise, but at the discounted rates. We did the picnic thing at the park, and the nighttime attraction sights at the South Sea Port. We did all things pleasant and affordable. It wasn't that I couldn't afford it, cause I had at least 58,000 in savings left and was virtually debt free, but I was also very money conscience. I was short of being scrooge without the mean-spirit. And then so was Carla. She was the type of woman you'd let handle your finances. As far as I know though, I never sensed any concerns of whether I was broke or not from her. She just never once came off as materialistic, which is a trait I naturally look out for in a woman. Call that obstinate of me, but it is what it is. So indeed, when it came to theater & fine arts, we took in a home video.

Sonja did keep calling, to my surprise. Or not. There were many times we would all be at the bar, and sure enough she would spot me with Carla. She would play it off as if it was nothing, but I could sense the greenness in her eyes. To be fair, Sonja and I would often talk on the phone as if we were dating, which is weird, cause up until that point we never went out and got intimate. She'd reveal to me all sorts of shit that I probably would've cared more about if we were actually together, but I didn't like to waste time. I made it clear, in not so many words, that I'm the type of guy that is not into keeping women around as hang out buddies. Sure we could talk, but if we're not getting intimate that's as far as it goes. No need to see you much. It might've seemed a harsh philosophy, but I was just trying to be truthful. I did keep in mind that this was Grip's ex. But I also had to keep in mind that she was probably just as murderous as he was. I couldn't get around the fact that she set that guy up in T's meeting charade. Who knew what else she was capable of? At least that is what I should've taken into consideration. Being the man that I am however, I finally couldn't resist her body any longer. I have never seen such a cute 'shortie' with an ass so fat, and thighs so thick. She shows up in front my door unannounced and was wearing some dress shit that took me back to when I first met her at the 'Ballahz Ballroom Ball 99'. Common sense rushed out of my head and testosterone filled the other. I took her instantly. That was one of a few times that I slept with her. That too also marked the beginning of trouble.

Chapter VII – ...And your enemies closer.

The news can be so depressing. There on the television it plays, over and over again like a bad nightmare. 6'oclock news. 8'olock news. 10'oclock news. And all the briefings in between. They say the Police are finding new leads and evidence that will bring the suspect in the double slayings of two dealership owners and the shooting of an off duty cop. The Mayor and the commissioner are both vowing to bring this vile perpetrator to justice. A healthy bounty is constantly flashing across the screen as to solicit any one with the information to bring this to an end. "Ugh", I sigh to myself every time I have to be reminded of it. When will the media attention from this going to die? If I had wings I would fly. I turn the television off and slump down into my one-seater couch. If I could just go away. Fade. Go to where? Perhaps I should turn myself in. Excuse me... While I get lost in thought... ... ... Zzzzz.

RING!! RING!!

Hm? My eyes open wearily. How long have I passed out from sleep? My eyes shift lazily to the clock on the wall. It's 1:34am. Almost 3 hours? The sleep felt longer.

RING!! RING!!

"Aww", I mumble to myself as I reach over to the phone. Who the fuck is this at this time? "Hello, Non speaking".
    "Hey sup boo? It's Sonja?"
    "Oh", I'm more up now. "Sup?"
    "Nothing much. It sounds like I woke you?"
    "You did."

"Good," She laughs and continues. "So I need you to come over. I wanna talk to you."

"Ok cool. Give me a moment to get ready."
I'm cruising over to another section in Brooklyn thinking I'm gonna get laid and instead, walk into a soap opera. We're on opposite ends of the couch facing each other, as I'm rock hard and listening to gossip.

"Come over this way," I beckon. "Why are you sitting all the way over there?"

She protests.

"Listen, Non. This you want to know. Pipe is still badmouthing you."

I sigh. "Pipe. What's he saying now?!

"He's saying how you think you're the shit. Going around telling people how you're plotting to take out Trevor and takeover. Trying to get the people against you. I know none of that shit is true. Right?"

"Whaddya mean right? Of course not! Ugh." I get up out of my seat pissed now. "What the fuck is it with this nigga?! Why he keep trying to bait me and shit? And I mean, damn, if I wasn't gonna get no pussy, couldn't you have told me this shit over the phone? Fuck."

She shoots a look at me and I know that I've crossed the line.

"Wait a minute muthaphucka. I never said it was that type of party in the first place."

"Well it's the middle of the night. What else could I assume?"

"You should assume that if I called you over here for something besides sex, then it's important. Besides Mann trying to kick it to that bitch you keep.."

"What?!" I interrupt. "What bitch? My Carla?!"

"Yes, your bitch," she stubbornly affirms.

"Don't call her that please."

"You got other things to worry about besides that. Guess who wanted me to set you up so they could put a bullet behind your cute skull?"

"Cute skull? Wh.. What the fuck you saying? Pipe wants me dead?"

"Pipe and Mann. I was supposed to call you out to the seaport late late night after closing. Get on a boat romantic like. Let you throw a few drinks in your system. Then next thing, you weighted down in the water. No trace. Nobody know nothing."

I pause to take all this in.

"You're serious?" I paused again. "Yo, you are one treacherous broad. The fuck happened to your childhood?"

"The fuck happened to yours?" she shot back sarcastically.

"Ok. Let me think." My mind was racing. I even wondered if this was a setup itself. I stare at Sonja. "I don't know why your 'Delilah like ways' is turning me on right now."

She seductively approaches me, "If I were Delilah you'd be dead by now."

We fall into bed and I blow her back out the rest of that night.

The Next day, back at my home in my solitude, I had pause for many thoughts and reached one conclusion. Pipe is a one track minded animal. I am going to brutally murder him so terribly, that he's going to get flashbacks of it in hell. I'm also going to send Mann with him for company.

We're coming into the year 2006. It's the beginning of the December and I want to see the New Year. The Day is Saturday. The time is 4pm. The sound to Lennon's, 'Happy X-Mas (War is over)' is playing in the background. Pipe is unloading groceries from the back of his sports utility vehicle. His wife calls out to him from the door way. He responds back to her in an irritated manner. I can't make out what they're saying. He leaves the back of the SUV open as he lugs grocery bags in both hands into his home. I quietly make my way down to his vehicle and creep into the rear. I hear him returning back. He appears to be complaining to his wife.

"I'll be back later. I don't have the time for this shit," he exclaims to his wife, as he shuts the back of his vehicle and gets into the driver seat. He pulls off unaware that I'm somewhere in the back seat.

The Christmas song is still playing when Pipe shuts it off.

"The Fuck," he mumbles to himself.

As he approaches a stop light; a deafening sound. BLAM!! I waste no time.

"AAAGH!" yelled out Pipe, in both agony and horror. I had sent one right into his right knee. I lunge forward and shift the gear into park, while simultaneously yoking him with my left arm around his neck from behind the driver seat. My right hand is still on the trigger of my Glock 19 and pressed against his head.

"This is a car-jacking bitch!" I announce in a raspy voice, in an attempt to disguise myself. "Drive."

"I... I can't. Mah... My leg!"

"Drive or Die." I tighten my hold. The horns are blowing with impatient and oblivious motorist behind us as the light turned green. Pipe makes an agonizing try and gets the car moving. "Turn here." I know his area well, as I already scoped it out. We pull into a quiet lot.

"Yo, yo please man. Just take the car."

"Oh relax man," I assure him, undisguising my voice.

"Oh shit!" he panics, trying to break free.

"Relax Pipe. I bench 295lbs and you're injured. You're not going anywhere."

"What the fuck man?! What's this about?"

"It's about me and you. I mean c'mon man, why would you think to play someone like me? You already know what I am."

"Fuck man." The nervousness ever creeping into his voice to a stutter. "Ok man. L-L-look man… What ever that bitch told you is a lie man. She scheming man…"

"Wh-wh-what bitch?" I interrupt mockingly.

"C'mon man." He gasps to catch his breath. "The bitch man. You know who I' talking about man."

"Oh her? How do you know about that anyway?"

"C'mon man…"

"You know what Pipe? I should have bodied you just for giving me attitude in the past. But seeing how we have history, I'm gonna let this slide. Nah mean? It's your boy I want. Mann. I heard he put yall up to that shit."

"Yo. Straight up. That nigga Mann is the one with all that drama man."

"I know. I know. I been peeped his style. Where he stay at yo?"

"Yo. He's always at Utica and Gates, at the Jamaican spot."

"Oh alright. Word."

"Fuck that nigga man. It was him talking all that shit."

"You got it." I release my hold.

"Damn dukes." He moans in pain, hunched over and rocking back and forth; both hands nursing his damaged knee. "You coming through at me all hard and shit."

"Forget all that. If I let you live, you gotta swear by Org code not to take this the hard way."

"Man, go head nigga." Pipes pain slowly transforms to anger. "You come to where I live with my wife there and all. You carjack my shit. Put a hole in my muthaphuckin knee… and now you want me to let that shit ride." He sucks his teeth. "Man just go head with that man."

"Ok. Ok. Just drive before I change my mind."

"Man what the FUCK I need to drive for man!?" he yells out. "You done with me, just leave me here."

He shoots me a wicked screw face.

"You're right Pipe." I hop out of the car and he pulls off instantly.

As Pipe pulls back up to his house, his wife runs outside to help him, phone in her hand. Pipe staggers out the car with his cell phone in his left hand.

"Oh My God! Oh my God!" she exclaims hysterically. "I called the ambulance!"

"Go back inside and get my shit together!" he bellows.

She complies, as he staggers on his left leg towards the door. Once there, he leans against his doorway and pauses to get a better footing. Then a familiar voice from a masked man remarks from behind.

"Hey Pipe… On second thought…" BLAM! A round straight to his turning head. He lays there convulsing. The masked man steps over him. BLAM-BLAM-BLAM-BLAM in rapid succession. The masked man flees in an unknown direction.

Enters the wife into the scene in full scream mode.

2 Days later at the park.

"You wanted to see me T?"

"Yeah. Who told you Non? Who authorized you to hit Pipe?"

"I didn't"

"You didn't?" He searches my face.

I could lie no longer. Not to T. I felt I was above that now.

"Yeah, I did. So what? Him and Mann was plotting to kill me. And fuck it, Mann's next. He's next. You wanna ask did I kill him. Hmpf. Ya damn right nigga. It's not like... like I could've come to you... the guys... I looked out for myself. I look out for me!"

T did not respond at all. He just looked away towards the floor. And there it was; 20 long seconds of deafening silence. He looked at me for a moment and then just left the scene. I suppose I should not have sounded so hostile. But I was tired. I was tired of all this. The Org. The crew. Trevor. Myself. The work. Everything. About the only person I could tolerate anymore was Carla. I know...! I'll get Carla to go away with me to Canada. Start a new life somewhere.

But where was she? I placed several calls to her and got no response. I went to her apartment several times, but no one answered. First, I was thinking that she just wanted her space. But why? No. We seemed to be getting along just fine with no signs of conflict. So nah, that couldn't be it. By day four, I was asking myself, 'Did she break up with me?! Shit." I slammed down the phone; my annoyance mixed with concern. By the time week one was over with, I had entertained the thought that she could've very well had been kidnapped and murdered. By week two I had convinced myself that it was more than likely probable that the worst in fact did happen. I shuddered. No. No way not my angel. I headed back to her apartment.

When I knocked and there was once again no answer, I broke my way in, shoulder to the door. I figured, fuck it. This was an emergency. If she's in danger then of course it's worth it. If not, then she'll at least know not to fuck around and ignore me when I'm trying to reach her. And if that's the case – fuck her anyway.

The scene in her room was eerily quiet. Nothing seemed too out of the ordinary, but it had a certain air about it; as though it's been empty for awhile. Every room I checked seemed like remnants of an area once filled with life – no more. They must've kidnapped her. What makes me think this? Just a feeling. I know what I'm involved in and I know how we roll. If my lifestyle has endangered Carla in any way, how could I forgive myself?

Dusk is setting in, darkening the unlit living room of where I still find myself sitting on Carla's sofa.

"Ok," I sigh to myself, as I look at the clock on the coffee table and determine that it's not my imagination. Carla's not coming home and something is definitely up. I don't fancy much this helpless feeling; not knowing where to turn or who to trust. Normally the answers were provided for me through my orders and I would execute them. This was different now. I couldn't turn to Trevor anymore. I wasn't naïve. I knew that I had pissed him off. Besides the fact that he no longer appeared to be the type of person who would concern himself with the lost love of another, what the fuck did he know anyway? What if he had something to do with this? Could he be that pissed off? Could he be out to get me? Then my mind went off on a tangent. What if I just take T out of the equation? I could just Ice – T and it's a rap! I could run this shit and keep everybody in line. Then my cell phone rumbled. Speak of the Muthaphuckin devil…

"Trevor, sup?"

"Sup Non? Make it over here. I've got something."

"Sure thing."

***

I'm cruising down the FDR highway listening to 'Hand on the Pump', by Cypress. Look at that view. New York City always had a beautiful view at night; with all the lights. The traffic is nice and spaced for a change. Within 25 minutes I pull up to the bar and turn off the engine. My seatbelt slides off at the click and I crack open my door to get out when a masked man jumps into the passenger side of my car and jams something into my ribs.

"This is a stick up nigga!"

"Oh shit!" I panic, throwing my hands on the steering wheel. The masked man laughs out hysterically and I instantly know who it is.

"What the fuck man?!" I breathe a sigh of relief with my hands on my chest. "You trying to give me a heart attack?"

Trevor only responds, still chuckling a bit. "I got a job for ya man."

"Oh yeah? What?

-The First Job-

"Tony the Tomahawk Montana. You heard of him?"

"Yeah, I know who he is. Seen his face before. He's the high profile vicious muthaphucka."

"Yeah him. I want you to do your thing."

"My thing," I paused to figure out how I should tell T that I don't want this to be my thing anymore. "Hey Trevor, about that man, I want out."

"What?"

"Yeah, I want out of this. As in I don't want to do this anymore. I want out and please tell me it doesn't involve me having to get whacked."

"Hm," Trevor pauses for a moment. "You know this is a surprise Non. I mean, what you gonna do out there? You sure you don't mind being a janitor? It's easy to forget how hard it is out there when you're living the life."

"That's just it. This isn't a life for me anymore. Look…" I take out some city job listing from my glove compartment. "they are giving the test for sanitation. I'm going to take it."

"You're not thinking Non. There's a waiting list for those test going up to 4 years. What you gonna wait 4 years to make a mediocre wage? In the meantime, good luck at McDonalds huh?"

"Look," I take a breath to reduce my growing agitation. "I have that worked out. Whatever I do, at least I'll be able to sleep better at night."

"And the Police? That cop? You forgot about that?"

"About what? Trevor, I hope to the heavens you're not wearing a wire."

"A what? Don't even fix your mouth to come at me like that again."

"Or what? What T?" I couldn't keep my temper any longer. "This is my life. My trauma. You don't give a fuck about me, or my problems. All you care about is your image to these goons. Meanwhile I'm your family. Me! And I got to make a fucking appointment just to talk to you."

There was that cursed uncomfortable tense silence again. We search each other's expression. Trevor looked blank. He just lit up a blunt from his coat, took a pull and looked out the window.

"You want out Non? You got it. Once you leave though, you can't come back."

"I won't."

"But, I do want you to do this job. Make your last bread and after that, it's done."

"Let me hit that," I motioned over to T for the blunt, as he passes it. I take a few drags. "This Nigga

'Texas'… he's kinda connected. I'm going to need people."

"Nah, just you. He's not protected like that."
"Ok."

Trevor starts to make his way out of the car.
"Oh T, one more thing."
"Yeah."
"You heard from Carla?"

"Please. Fuck I know about your bitches? Just get the job done, or you're leaving this thing a different way."

"Yeah? Well, if this is a setup, so are you nigga," I retort back as Trevor exits my vehicle and walks off.

I surprised myself with that last comment. I was a fed up homicidal mild mannered sociopath, who'd already put in some real grizzly work. The fuck did I care about what anyone thought anymore; including Trevor. Off I went to prepare.

-The Aftermath of the First Job-

<We know how it all went down; the hit against Tony Texas. That was my introduction into how I got here. Where's here? Read on. >

I'm thinking of the past event with Texas. That Fucking Trevor. He told me… he assured me there were no needs for back up. He told me that Tony always rolled light. But Tony didn't roll light that night. In fact, I did some street research and found that Tony never rolled light. Tony the Tomahawk Texas was like a celebrity criminal. Like a Don. He was also high profile, so of course he'd always roll with an entourage. Why was I not thinking of that before? And after that insane gun battle, the one I ended up coming ill prepared for; the one where I could've and should've easily been killed; finally dawned on me that maybe Trevor was setting me up to get killed. It made sense. He would've been plotting this then since before I told him I wanted out. That motherfucker then would've known all along that he wanted me iced. That sonofabitch. I bet he was so tickled inside when I told him that I wanted out. He was probably thinking, 'yeah, you'll get out alright!' Fucking snake. But wait, let me slow down. Why just not have the crew do me in? And then to make matters worse...

'Knock – Knock'

A knock at the door. I peek through the peep hole. It's the law! Shit. Should I run out the back? Shit! Think! Wait. I take a deep breath. If they were coming for me on this thing, then they'd have been busting in the door with a warrant and a team. No, it was just two detectives. C'mon Non, get it together and put yourself in an innocent state of mind. I open the door.

"Hello?"

"Hello. You are Shannon Samuel correct?"

"Yes sirs, Officers..." I lean forward to see if any identification of their names.

"We're Detectives Scott and Detective Curwen of the New York City Police department. May we come in?"

"Uh, one sec. I'm in my boxers. Let me just throw on my pants."

I shut the door locked. Ok think. We had a few Officers that were 'on the take' indulge us before. What was it that was said...? Ah. I throw on a pair of jeans and went back to the door. I open the door, step out and pull it locked behind me.

"Now, where were we?" I inquire, acting fully oblivious.

"Sir," one continues. "Is there any reason you locked yourself out?"

"Oh, I'm not locked out sir. I have a key."

We all stare at each other for a moment. And then it continues.

"We would like you to come down and answer a few questions."

"About?"

Then the other Officer, Detective Curwen, who was seemingly shorter tempered interjected, "Listen. Everyone knows about the big shooting of Tony Texas the other night."

"I've heard something about that. Yes," I responded concerned.

He continues, "Yeah, well. There was a car taken from a victim later found not far from a train station. Guess what? Guess who's on the station camera?"

"Wow. What's your name again?"

"Detective Curwen."

"Well, Detective Curwen, I'm sure it's just coincidence."

"Oh yeah?" he turns to his partner and they kind of grin to each other. "Tell you what... We think you should come with us."

"I follow you guys. I do. Tell you what though, is there a warrant for my arrest? I mean, just for my own knowledge."

"No."

"Ok, well... I won't fight you. I don't believe in fighting the Police. But I do know this... You don't have enough for an arrest. I mean, unless riding the train is a crime. I won't answer any of your questions without representation regardless. I'm just too afraid to get wrongly accused. You know a lot of innocent people are in prison. I just don't want to waste you guy's time."

We all stare at each other again for a moment.

"This one has something to hide," states Detective Scott to his partner, all the while never breaking his glare at me.

"It would appear so," replies Detective Curwen. "Tell you what," he continues   with a smile. "We are going to be visiting you again really soon."

I smile back.

"Detective Curwen. That smile makes you a real handsome man."

They walk back to their 'unmarked RMP' car with a look of disgust. As soon as they drive off I go back into my domain; Nervous. Panic mode sets in again. They're going to get a warrant. They're going to tear this place apart. I don't have much time. Focus. I need to get with Trevor and get this finalized.

I attempted to place several calls to Trevor. No answer. I didn't feel comfortable going to his house just yet. Didn't feel safe. I decided to call Sonja.

RING!

The phone rings, but no answer. I call back right after. I mean what the fuck? Lately it's like I can't reach no...

"Hello," say Sonja from the other end.

"Sonja! Sonja, listen. I'm looking for T. It's important and I can't trust no one else. Not even T. Or, I think I can trust him, but I want to be sure. I need to be sure Sonja. So please, I need to get with T."

"Slow down," she responds. "Be easy. I just spoke to T..."

"What he say?" I interrupt. No time for small talk.

"Damn you eager."

"Sonja!"

"Ok, ok. Listen. He says shit is falling apart and he don't know who to trust. There's a lot going on Non."

"Well where is he Gottdammit?!"

"I can't tell you over the phone. Meet me at my place."

"Damn Sonja. How I don't know where he at, but you do?" I pause. "You fucking him?"

"What?!"

"Never mind. I'm on my way."

I race up the block doing 83...

<There's no thought going on in my mind's eye right now. I got to get to Sonja.>

When I get near her place I call, but no answer.

"Fucking unreliable," I mutter to myself.

I notice somebody peek around the corner and disappear again. Probably nothing, but it's getting dark. That and her well to do brownstone neighborhood is already creepy enough. Sonja's block is nestled in the rear of the Brooklyn Promenade. There isn't too much pedestrian traffic in the back of the Promenade when it gets dark.

I step out of the car with my cell phone to my ear.

"Hello?" Sonja finally answers.

"Sonja. Sup? Let me in."

"I'm not coming down the stairs," she protests. I just got out of the shower."

"Oh word?" I respond, thoughts of perversion dancing around in my head. Nah. I collect myself. Focus. No time to be thinking about Punanny. "Throw the key down then?"

A minute passes by before her window opens up and a key comes flying out of it. I'm thinking, 'Ok, she got out the shower and she doesn't want to catch a draft.' I make my way up the outside brownstone stairs, unlock the front door and push it open. Right before I fully step in, I lean my head back to look up, to make certain that she at least knew I got the key alright. Coincidentally, the light from the window went out that instant. 'Nice,' I'm thinking. She must be setting the mood for some much needed intimate release.

I enter onto the first floor hallway landing and can tell that the 3rd floor light must've blew, because the landing after the first flight of steps; its' lights are faded. Damn. I've always been leery about the dark. As I'm about to continue up to the 2nd floor, there was a call on my cell phone. I stop. I never talk on cell phones and climb stairs. Call me weird. But It's Sonja.

"Sup," I answer. "I'm already on my way up."

"Hurry up then," she responds impatiently. "I left the door cracked open and it's letting all the cold air in."

"Ok, ok," I responded.

"One more thing."

"What's that?"

"Stay on the phone with me," she says in a playful tone.

I laugh to myself. I already know. "Oh word? You seriously setting the mood huh?"

"You know it... but... I don't hear you coming up the stairs. Sup?"

"What? Oh, nah girl. I don't go up the stairs and talk at the same time."

"What?" she responds, now in an annoyed tone. "That's the dumbest shit... Whateva. Just hurry up." She hangs up the cell. Typical emotional roller coaster shit with her. No wonder this chick is so psychotic.

But then it hit me! Then it Mutha Fuckin hit me! Oh shit! What if this is a... I pull out the cell and hit the redial button. No answer. Just ringing. Then I hear another ring. It must be from her cell, only it's getting closer. I start to sweat. This gotta be a setup. Oh shit again! What if it's a setup?! I shut the phone off and dump it in my coat pocket. I still never even got half way up the first flight of stairs. But I damn sure slid the 'sawed-off' shotgun from out of my 'Goose.' Whateva Bitch, you not getting me!

I back down the stairs and hunch down into a corner. I'm at the main inner doorway. Waiting. Nothing. Not one movement and not one sound. I'm almost paralyzed with fear right now. I'm believing – Death was up those stairs. There's a hit squad waiting for me. Only the heavens know where. Or hell. My Fear is overcome with the calmness of knowing that the death of me can finally bring an end to all this tension. But fuck that. Not

141

in this building. I slide in between the inner and the main doors. Still crouched down, I reached up for the main door knob with my right hand, still holding the shotgun with my left and crack it open. I then slowly push the main door further open with my foot. I take the quickest peak through the outer glass of the main door, simultaneously ducking back down. I swivel to look through the inner door's glass, to make sure whomever wasn't coming down the stairs behind me. I know that I can't stay playing around between these two doors. I hide the shotgun under my arm and bust out the front door, falling down the outer stairs and expecting a barrage of shots. But nothing. I prop myself up against a tree and wait for it. Still nothing. I stand up, still a bit hunched over.

The scenery is quiet and deserted. What the fuck? Still leery, I correct my posture and walk carefully to my auto. Just as I breathed a sigh of relief, I noticed a dark Suburban vehicle pull up down the block; its' windows tinted. And so it just sits there. I turn my head and look down the other end of the block and spy a dude with a hoodie pulled over his head, looking downwards. I can only make out that he's wearing shades. 'This is it' I'm thinking. What if I'm wrong though? What if it's just a jeep sitting on the corner and the guy walking up is just a passerby shielding himself from the unusually chilly weather for this time? Maybe I'm just paranoid this whole time. But if I don't use some discernment soon and this is in fact a hit, then I'm no longer. Fuck it! If I'm wrong, then wrong place – wrong time. I've done worse.

I up the shotgun and let off a blast towards the Suburban. BRAHMM! I then run in the opposite direction, but choosing the street rather than the sidewalk, as to use the parked cars for cover. I still wanted to stay close. The man with the hoodie attempted to brace himself, but instead just got blasted with my sidearm. Sure enough he had a piece in his hand. The Suburban swings down the block towards me and I continue to dash away. I swing the corner and take cover a few parked cars behind. Fuck that. I'm not getting chased til' I get shot in the back. Let's go. As the suburban swings the corner after me, I pop up and unload a shot into the windshield. CRACK!! That's slug two. The suburban veers right and crashes into a row of parked cars, opposite from where I was positioned. The door pops open and the driver staggers out hunched over. He collapses to the pavement as though out of the fight. Yeah fuck head! The others exit the wreck disoriented and blasting wildly. I take cover, drop the sawed off, pull out two semi – auto 9mm and engage. I'm not about wasting shots either. I once again use the parked cars to my advantage and take off around the corner. Illusion. I instantly pop back out, using the nearby rounding corner of the building for what cover it would provide, catching any mutha fuckas who was on my tail, left out in the open. BLOK BLOK BLOK…!! Well aimed adrenaline crushing upper torso and head shots, causing a chain reaction – and one by one they all start to drop. And so on. I felt like a conductor orchestrating a volley of gunfire towards my audience. The last one thought he would be stealth and adopt my style by creeping along the parked cars on the opposite end. He's the only one still upright. We go at it. Soon nothing. I peer and throw a few shots. Still nothing, but he's still scurrying excitedly. I pop up and make my way towards his location – two pistols up. He makes a dash for the wrecked Suburban in a panic with the gun still in his hand. I know what that meant. Would you believe this killer came to a gunfight without enough ammo? The nerve. BLOK BLOK goes the rounds into his bottom half and he falls against the truck.

"Oh," I approach with a sinister laugh. "So you thought you were gonna just come out here and mop a nigga up 1-2-3 like huh?" He staggers to keep himself up;

one arm against the truck, the other up in mercy. "Nah, muthaphucka! No mercy!"

BLOK BLOK BLOK BLOK.

Go in peace.

I look over at the remaining guys on the ground and throw a few slugs into em', just to be certain. I'm on a murderous high now. I'm going back to the building. I turn the corner to see two goons and Sonja run out of her building and up to an Oldsmobile that a third goon was driving, totally unaware that anyone would be mad enough to return to the beginning of an inevitable crime scene. I just gotta do them before the Police arrive. I was already armored. I've been paranoid since I dropped Texas. However, I couldn't just risk another brazen gun battle with them where I'm out numbered. My luck would eventually run out. I know. I'll wait until they're all in the car. And sure enough, as they all rush into the car, I don't give them a moment to even close all doors. I run up alongside of their vehicle, fully blazing. That part was easy. I just kept shooting until everyone stopped moving. The driver first. Sonja I didn't shoot. I needed her; wanted her alive.

Sonja was in the rear driver's side seat suffering form the shock and daze.

"Come out," I ordered. She didn't respond. Didn't even turn to face me. "Alright, I'll just help myself." I grab her by her hair and yank her out. "Get the fuck outta the car," I snort. She falls to the ground. "I haven't got much time Sonja, tell me who and I'll let you live, in the name of our history."

She looks up at me, still in a daze.

"T... Trevor."

"You sure?"

"Yeah. Yes," she gasps.

"Thanks babe." I level the gun towards her head and blow it away. BLOK!

***

Now, if I can just get to Trevor, before he gets word that his plan did not work. Perhaps then we can rectify this problem. I get back in my vehicle and I head straight there.

Chapter VIII – And so it goes.

The radio is playing, 'I don't care anymore', by Phil Collins. Fitting. I take the Brooklyn Bridge into Manhattan for the Holland Tunnel. Man these city lights are beautiful.

When I did pull up to his area, I made sure to park a few blocks away. If dude really does want me dead, then walking up his front porch and announcing myself might only prove detrimental. No. I creep cautiously up the block to the house. His car is not there and the lights are out. I'm thinking, 'not again.' But I still have the key to his place on my key chain. Go figure. I take out one of my reloaded pistols and lower it to against my leg. I slowly unlock and push open the door. I've lived there before, so I know the place. After fully clearing the whole pad, I realize that T just hasn't gotten here yet. I keep the lights out and wait on the couch.

A little over 1hour pasts and I hear a key at the door. It's Trevor and he's alone. The lights go on and he hurriedly comes through his living area with a stack of his postal mail in one hand.

"Sup T?" I greet.

He instantly jumps back startled. "What the fuck?!"

"Ha ha. I got you back. Remember when we was in the car?"

He stares at me. Of course he already knows it's me, but he seemed panicked.

"Yeah, I remember. Sup?" he answered quietly.

I waste no time getting to the matter.

"The fuck yo? You want me dead?"

"The gun for Non?"

"What you think T? Just answer the fucking question."

"What's there to answer Non? Yes. Yes, I put a hit out on you."

I pause, taken aback by Trevor's cold bluntness. I was even partially hurt.

"Oh word cousin? Well... I figured that much. I figured that on my own." I take a breath. "Just tell me why, so we can get this over with."

Trevor places the mail down on the table with a look of resignation. He begins,

"I had to give you up Non. The Org said so. Ever since the incident with the cop. You fucked up. You fucked up royally, and it was felt that you should be dealt with before you were caught." He pauses and takes a seat. "I mean, I was in a compromising position. They catch you – you implicate me – I implicate them. See what I mean? You get caught, I'm dead. I did bring you in you know? Or did you forget? Anyhow, I'm the only thing that links them. It's just that simple."

I don't say a word, I'm just listening. He continues.

"Something went wrong though. Somebody leaked to the Feds and I got pinched. I had to..."

"Enough," I interrupt, standing myself up from the couch. "Next, you're gonna tell me you're an informant." I search his face and he only stares back in a look of defeat. "No way man not you. Not you T." He does not respond. Wow. Sigh. "Know what cousin, it doesn't even matter anymore."

"What you gonna do family? You're going to kill me? You're going to kill the flesh and blood that took you in from disparity? The one that brought you in from despair? The one that brought you into all of this?

To which my reply, "I couldn't do this to you cousin no matter what. That is under normal circumstances. But, you did try to kill me Trevor. And for that reason, yes. Yes, I am going to kill you now."

"Fuck You!" he declares, as he makes a dash for the kitchen.

He doesn't get that far before I release a few rounds into his back, using the couch pillow to muffle the sounds. 'Kak Kak Kak' – in rapid succession. And there he lay in the doorway, halfway between the kitchen and the living room. He's faced down and he's not moving, but I can hear him struggling to breath. I walk over and give him a mercy killing - POP - that is one more slug to the back of his head. It's finished. A sickening feeling of remorse grips my stomach for a moment. It overtakes me. The tears. It felt surreal; me standing in the very house that we shared together as brothers. Now we were eternally parted as enemies. That hurted. It's also over for me. It is a must that I retreat back to the house and get my emergency fugitive backpack and flee the country. First thing in the morning.

***

I wake up in my own pad at around 5am. I grab my duffle bag and backpack. It has all my clothes, documents and $40,000 cash. I didn't like banks much, but I did have another $25,000 in funds placed there in case my place caught on fire. I had this plan setup. I would drive to Canada and live in peace and obscurity.

The End.

NOT →

All the fuck I had to do was get to the bank. I had
already set it up to where I'd pull my funds out with no
problems. Banks can act silly when you want to take
money out of that magnitude; even if it's yours. But I got
through that with no sweat.

I parked my car somewhere on a quiet block in
LIC Queens with the idea of taking the subway to the Port
Authority. I figure out the safer the better. The weather
was cold, so I had a reason to wear a black scarf over my
nose and mouth; complete with a dark set of shades
without raising a hint of curiosity. I didn't want my car no
where near the Port Authority either. Sure I would've
preferred to drive, but I didn't need my Tag caught on any
interstate Toll booth camera. Call me careful.

Sigh… But of course, Murphy's Law.

I'm taking my bags out of the car, when almost as
in slow motion, an unmarked Police Impala jumps up on
the side walk. Behind that one is the same, followed by at
least two more Police cruisers. I automatically jump over
my car and make a dash for any better cover across the
street. I had a split second decision to make. Shoot it out
or get taken in. They were too close and obviously had a
sting setup, so outrunning them was out of the question. I
would likely die in a shootout with the Police, whether
now or later. Still, it was the only thing I knew how to do
best. It was by now instinctual. I hear a shout behind me
from a familiar voice.

"MR SAMUEL!" shouted Detective Scott.

In one of the Impalas' were the same two
Detectives from previous. Seems they made good on their
promise to see me again. I respond by taking cover
behind a car that was at a stoplight and opening fire with
the only gun I had.

BLAM BLAM - <continuous rapid fire.>

It was deafening. I unsuccessfully tried to muscle the surprised citizen, whose car I was using for cover, out of his car. He responded by stepping on the gas and pulling off. This sent me rolling into the middle of the street and wide open. Rounds are hitting my legs and arms as I stagger back up and duck into a nearby public building.

"AAGH," I scream out in pain.

I'm out gunned and I know it. I hurriedly limp through a few alarmed citizens and bust out the back of the building. My gun is still in my hand. Never will I part with it. Or so I thought. I don't even get a chance to raise my gun before my hand seemingly explodes. Their fucking cavalry showed up already there and the shots coming from them ripped through and blew me backwards into the building lobby. *Such terrible pain.* The Police run over to me, their guns drawn. I'm thinking, 'Just kill me now please.' They get blurry and I fade away. I think I'm Dead.

***

When I come to, I learn that I'm a high profile prisoner in custody at the hospital. It's where I'm healing, while waiting to recuperate in time for my trial. I'm handcuffed to the hospital bed and there are always at least two Police Officers guarding my room. By the time of the trial, I was in a court room painted as one of the key masterminds behind this huge murderous enterprise. It's definitely bad enough to be on trial for shooting at Law Enforcement Officers, but they were talking about some RICO shit. (Racketeering Influenced Corrupt Organization) And I never ran anything. There were testimonies from people I didn't even remember existed. In fact, I don't even think I met half of them. But I was in total shock when an FBI agent took the stand. It was fucking Manuel! Mann! 'Oh shit' I thought to myself. I had forgotten all about taking care of him.

They knew everything. Funny, didn't hear much about the Org though. Turns out, there was no Org. Not like I envisioned it anyway. I thought we were taking orders from some shadow government group full of old bitter muthaphuckas. Space shit. Turns out that the Org was just us; the various crews that was down with our thing. The leaders of these crews kept that a secret from everyone – including us. That's how they kept order. If one died, another stepped up and was informed. Ran pretty structured too. Credit. Still don't know how it started though.

They knew about several hits; about the Tony Texas hit; the dealership murders and the wounded cop. I'm a fucking dead man. They even played a recording of Trevor ordering me to whack Texas and implementing me with the wounded cop, who happened to be at my trial with a slew of other officers by the way. Fucking Trevor. That fucking Cain. He had a wire on that whole time. They made no link between me and the Sonja ordeal though, nor Trevor. I think they knew, just didn't have the evidence. Them not presenting it wouldn't do me any good though, not with what they already had on me.

Oh, I even found out what happened to Carla. She was never in danger. No. The authorities got to her and tried to leak her for what she knew. When they figured out that she knew nothing and was just an innocent party, they advised her of how dangerous I was and that it was beneficial for her to split town. So she did. Wow. Just like that, no consultation with me or anything. She could've tipped me to this whole shit. Instead, she ran off and is now in a more meaningful relationship with Agent Mann. I suppose I should be happy for her. Fucking Bitch. When it was all said and done, I was found guilty of all charges. It was finally time for sentencing. I stood tall before the man.

The Judge Read:

"Mr. Shannon Samuel, for you implication in a murderous organization that claimed several lives, as well as your brazen disregard for this society and the authority sworn to protect it… I sentence you to be removed to the custody of the U.S. Marshalls service for transportation to the 'Peoples High Security' prison/penitentiary for a term of 15 years to life."

There was a mix of both thunderous applause and disappointment, as the Judge banged his gavel and declared order. It wasn't that I had anyone on my side. It was just that people either thought the sentence was 'just', or not enough. I was actually relieved in a twisted way by the 15 – life sentencing. I expected two life sentences without the possibility of parole. I mean, I could be in there for life, or I could at least try after 15yrs to get out again. Maybe. When I was asked before if I had anything to say, I only responded that I was sorry.

But in actuality, inside I felt like shit. I now longed for those days when I was just Joe Blow citizen looking for a break. I know now that I was smart enough to make it legitimately in life eventually, but was just too angry and naïve. I have no one to blame, but myself. And it wasn't just me being here. It was my soul up for grabs. I allowed myself to become a monster. I took lives. I tried to justify that some deserved it; but there were some who didn't. Some who got caught in the crossfire of a violent world, whether through me or the crew I was representing. And for what? Money? When I think that I've tarnished my soul and fucked myself to likely a life sentence to hell on earth, while other folk out there made real money on just brain power, minus all that evil shit that I did, it sickens myself.

I am done.

I am escorted by the U.S. Marshalls out of the court house.

I am deserving of it.

Maybe somewhere in that steel nightmare, I can try to finally find peace.

THE END

22294816R00085

Made in the USA
Charleston, SC
15 September 2013